PRISONER OF WAR

PRISONER OF WAR
My secret journal

Squadron Leader B. Arct

Stalag Luft 1, Germany 1944-45

Webb & Bower
MICHAEL JOSEPH

ACKNOWLEDGEMENT
The publishers would like to thank Beryl Arct, Ryszard Arct,
Krystyna Mucko and Jeanne Skinner, Bohdan Arct's wife, son,
daughter and niece, who have made the publication
of this book possible

First published in Great Britain 1988 by
Webb & Bower (Publishers) Limited
9 Colleton Crescent, Exeter, Devon EX2 4BY
in association with Michael Joseph Limited
27 Wright's Lane, London W8 5TZ

Jacket design Vic Giolitto

Production Nick Facer / Rob Kendrew

Text and illustrations copyright © 1988 Beryl Arct, Ryszard Arct and Krystyna Mucko

British Library Cataloguing in Publication Data

Arct, B.
Prisoner of War: the secret log book of
Squadron Leader B. Arct, Stalag Luft 1,
Barth, Germany 1944-1945.
1. World War, 1939-1945 – Prisoners and
prisons, German 2. World War, 1939-1945 –
Personal narratives, British
I. Title
940.54'72'430924   D805.G3

ISBN 0-86350-229-6

Typeset in Great Britain by P&M Typesetting Ltd, Exeter

Colour reproduction by Peninsular Repro Service Ltd, Exeter

Printed and bound in Hong Kong by Mandarin Offset

Contents

Barth Hard Times

Publisher's Note

The page numbers from the original journal have been used. Where these are not consecutive this is not because anything has been left out but because this is how they appear in the original.

Preface

The majority of Bohdan Arct's works are factual accounts of the Second World War written to explain the Polish contribution to the Allied effort. They are illustrated with photographs and the proceeds in large part went to organizations for Polish airmen. This journal on the other hand was put together by Arct purely to amuse his fellow inmates and to provide release and relaxation for himself. Materials were scarce – witness the grey cardboard used in the centre section, spare time was precious, Arct was often exhausted by hunger, and the journal was at all times under threat of confiscation by the guards. Nevertheless, in nine months, he managed to invent and illustrate something which, forty-five years later, still has the power to entertain and arrest.

Arct took his "Log Book" with him when he left the camp and kept it with other mementoes of his war experiences, including an extensive diary in Polish covering the whole six years. But there was no thought of publishing it – for several reasons. Firstly, he and his family felt it was too personal to have a broad appeal, or for them to be happy about its publication; secondly, it was written in English (and from 1947 onwards they were living back in Poland); and lastly, it was too soon after the events it described.

Fourteen years after Arct's death however, and with the increasing public interest in diaries and facsimiles, the family decided the time was right to try and bring the journal to a wider audience, and they sent it to relatives in England. There, its merit and interest were immediately recognized.

The original was later presented by the family to the Imperial War Museum in London for safekeeping.

At the end of the narrative, on page 71, Arct says, "We woke up on the 1st of May [1945] with a strange feeling of freedom": they were indeed liberated. But it took a week for the chaos to subside and the evacuation of the men to begin. "Barth Hard Times Vol 1 No 1 Last 1", kindly brought to light by Harry de Belleroche, one of Arct's fellows in "Room 2", and included here at the end, was compiled by some of the other inmates during these last few days, which it describes. As a further example of irrepressible talent, it provides a fitting conclusion to the fascinating and vivid story of a POW.

Biography

Arct was born in Poland on 27 May 1914. His father was a Warsaw publisher and his mother a writer of books for children and young people. After finishing grammar school in 1932 he went on to flying school which he finished in 1934 with the rank of Flying Officer. In 1935 he became a student at the Warsaw Academy of Art. On 1 September 1939 he was mobilized as Liaison Officer in the Polish Air Force.

At the end of September, together with most other Polish pilots, he arrived in Romania where he was interned. In October, disguised in civilian clothing, he escaped to Marseilles. After being trained in France he was sent to North Africa to act as a flying instructor. In June 1940 he arrived in England.

After a short course in English he was posted to Ferry Pilots Pool, Kemble, and in the following year he transferred to Heston, where he trained as a fighter pilot on a Spitfire. A few months later he was posted to 306 Squadron in Exeter. In 1943, with a group of Polish pilots, he volunteered to go to North Africa, where he and the others fought alongside the British 145 Squadron.

On returning from North Africa he acted as Commander of B Flight in 303 Squadron. In 1944, during a rest period, he wrote his first book, *Chasing the Luftwaffe*. A few months later he was promoted to Squadron Leader of 316 Squadron; this squadron attacked the V1 bomb. On 6 September 1944, during a flight over Holland, his plane caught fire and he was forced to bale out. He was captured and taken to Stalag Luft 1 prisoner of war camp. It was during the seven months in this camp that he wrote what he called his "Log Book", *Prisoner of War*.

During his war service he received two important Polish decorations for bravery in the field, the *Virtuti Militari* and the *Krzyz Walecznych*, the latter awarded four times.

When the war was over he went back to England. In 1947, together with his wife and daughter, he returned to Poland, where life became very difficult. No work and serious financial problems led him into book illustration and in 1952 he left the town where he was living and settled in the country. Here he began to write book after book. In May 1973 he died suddenly of heart failure.

Because of the political situation his books were not published until 1956, but between 1952 and 1971 he wrote forty-three books. These have been translated from Polish into both German and English and, in the three languages, over four million copies have been printed and sold.

Oh I have slipped the surly bonds of earth
And danced the skies on laughter silvered wings
Sunward I've climbed and joined the tumbling mirth
Of sunsplit clouds and done a hundred things you have
Not dreamed of — wheeled and soared and spun high
In the sunlit silence.
Up, up the long, delirious burning blue
I've topped the windswept heights with ease
Where never larks or even eagles flew
Hovering there I've chased the shouting winds
Along the footless halls of air
And while with silent lifted mind
I've trod the high untrespassed sanctity of space
Put out my hand and touched the face of God.

THE STORY OPENS

-Do you believe in Gremlins?-No! Neither do I, but in my opinion nothing else could explain my involuntary and forcible visit to Goonland /country in Europe, sometimes called "Deutschland Kaput"/.

One sunny afternoon, on September 6th 1944, I found my= self leading eight Mu= stangs of my Squadron on an operational flight over Holland. As, unfor= tunately, I am still in Goonland writting these words, I cannot disclose the details of our trip or give any particulars of my operatio= nal records. Even mentionning the word "Goonland" would get me into serious trouble, probably 15 days in an uncomforta= ble, solitary cell, if did not hide this book well enough.

However, let's get back to the subject. Our flight was going entirely according to plan, until the moment, when I heard some strange noises in my engine. It seemed as if someone was striking

iron railings with a stick. A moment later the hand of the oil pressure gauge flicke= red and began to move slowly to the left.

I felt the perspi= ration pouring off my forehead. I knew then, that I would never re= turn to my base, as my aircraft had only a few minutes life left.

However, knowing that the Allied lines should be about loo mi= les to the South-west, I turned in that direction, warning my boys over

the radio, and asking them to escort me. I still had about lo.ooo feet on the altimeter, and, providing my engine kept going for some time, I still had a chance, with luck, to reach our front lines. I checked all the instruments, cocks, and controls in the cockpit, hoping to find the fault, but every= thing was correct. Unfortunately, there was little doubt that the defect was a major one, most probably one of the pistons had broken, and the engine, instead of roaring smoothly, was chugging and popping like an old chaff-cutter.

The oil pressure indicator dropped back until it regis= tered zero, where it remainded. Black smoke commenced pouring from the exhaust stubs, and, in spite of all efforts, I began to lose speed and height. I calculated briefly, that I should not reach our lines, but that I should probably have to land somewhere in the vicinity of the River Lek, which I could see distinctly ahead. I hoped to be able to make the other side of the river since it would be easier to escape from there. By now, the smoke was so thick, that I could

scarcely breathe. Occa= sionally, red flames bel= ched out of the exhaust, and the engine began to run intermittently. It was time I made my exit, but I still wanted to fly as long as possi= ble, in order to shorten

the distance between myself and the front lines.

At 2.000 feet I decided to bale out. The risk of for= ced landing on the Dutch fields, intersected by numerous dy= kes and rows of trees, was too great. I gave a final call on the radio:—"I am about to bale out. Cheerio. See you soon."—

A few seconds later I jettisoned the hood, unfastened my harness and simply stepped out of the aircraft. By this time the engine had stopped com= pletely and my Mustang was gliding noiselessly. I was vaguely aware that I hit something, but felt no pain at the time. Fe= verishly, I felt for the rip-cord and pulled it. Next moment I was falling through the air, terribly scared by a ridiculous thought, that the rip-cord had broken and my parachute would not open. Suddenly, I felt a terrific jerk, and a huge, white copula opened above my head. I had just enough time to look below and see a field of cabbages growing rapidly larger. The next second I hit the ground, was dragged along by the collapsing parachute, and then lay quietly among the big cabbage heads.

I was feeling somewhat dizzy, but pulled myself together, jettissoned my parachute, and leaped to my feet. I felt an agonizing pain around my ribs and nearly collapsed again. But there was no time

to lose. I looked around and saw a group of men, obviously Dutch peasants, wearing blue blouses. I walked towards them, with my hands pressed to my painful breast.

Our conversation was not a lengthy one. I only wanted to know where the Germans were and where I could hide. I gathered from their strange language that there were no Jerries in the vicinity, and that my best hiding place was a small copse some 1000 yards away. I decided to hide there

until the evening and then review the situation.

I lit a cigarette and staggered along slowly, the pain from my injured ribs preventing any rapid movement. In a few minutes I was under the shelter of the friendly trees. The

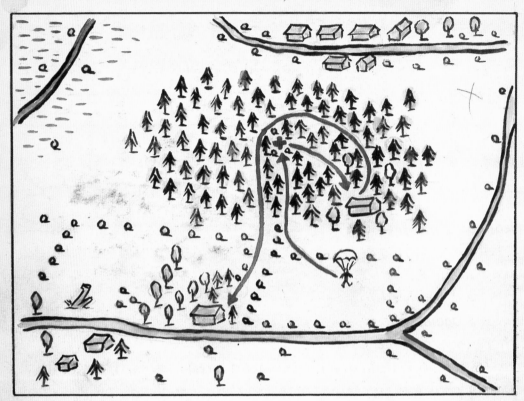

undergrowth, dense and thick, made an ideal hiding place, but after walking for about 500 yards, I emerged from the other side of the wood. In front of me, 100 yards away, was a village in which I could see German soldiers.

I turned back into the wood and made my way to the middle, where I found a small tree with foliage growing close to the ground. I crawled under the branches and lay down to rest and meditate. First I went through my pockets in order to destroy any papers which would be of value to the enemy, and then I examined my ribs. I came to the conclusion that I must have broken one when I was hit by the aircraft in baling out.

I opened my escape kit and examined the map of Holland. My plan was a simple one. I would lie in hiding until everything around was quiet, then find a farm where I could get some civilian clothes, and possibly contact the underground resistance movement, and commence walking towards the front line. To me this plan seemed simple enough, because the Germans were supposed to be pulling out of Holland, and I thought any Dutchman would assist an Allied airman. This was the information given by our Intelligence officers before take off.

I was trying to locate my exact position on the map, when I heard a heavy lorry approaching rapidly. I listened with bated breath, a strange sinking feeling in my stomach, as I heard numerous shouts and whistles, not more than 200 yards away. The hunt was on!!!

Another lorry followed the first and stopped on the opposite side of the wood. The Germans were obviously taking no risks, and intended to thoroughly comb the only possible hiding place in the area. They threw a cordon around the wood and commenced working inwards.

The voices were now so near that I could distinguish German words. Branches and twigs were cracking as the soldiers forced their way through the thick undergrowth. The sounds grew nearer and nearer, while I crouched under my little bush, wishing I could make myself invisible.

I held my breath as some twigs snapped a few yards away. Looking cautiously through the foliage I saw two bayonets and two pairs of heavy boots coming straight towards me. I thought the end had come, now, and my heart almost stopped beating as I watched those boots come so close that I could

have touched them. Then, suddenly, they turned aside, and I could hear them retreating, the sound growing fainter and fainter, until silence fell around me. I lay motionless under my blessed bush, my heart beating wildly.

The immediate danger had passed, but the Germans were still searching the wood, moving in all directions. Then, after about an hour, the whistles sounded again, somebody shouted loudly, and the lorries engines started. In a few minutes the sound of the retreating lorries died away. For the time being I was saved.

The wood once again

assumed a peaceful air. I heard birds singing and chirping while the fresh breeze gently moved the branches of the trees. Only in the distance could one hear the intermittent sound of exploding ammunition from my Mustang.

It was almost dusk when I left my hiding place and made for the edge of the wood. I did not dare to go towards the village where I had seen the soldiers, so I turned back towards the cabbage patch where I had landed. I stopped on the fringe of the wood and carefully surveyed the view. On my left there lay a farm half hidden by the trees, ahead of me was the cabbage patch with another farm in the distance, while some 1000 yards to my right I could see my aircraft with black smoke still rising from it. I considered it safest to try my luck at the first farm, because even if I did not succeed in achieving my object initially, I could easily return to the wood unobserved.

I could see no one in the vicinity, so I moved carefully forward and entered the farmyard through a gate. Everywhere was quiet and deserted, but, on approaching, I heard noises inside the house. I peered through the window and saw some five peasants sitting around a table eating their supper. I knocked on the door and entered.

My appearance must have given them quite a shock, because they were speechless for some minutes. I smiled painfully and tried to speak to them in German. Unfortunately, my knowledge of that awful language was very slight, but my wild gesticulating helped somewhat. The eldest peasant, whom I took to

be the father of the family, arose from the table and led me into another room, jabbering in Dutch, meantime, to a youngster who looked like his son. In the next room I tried to explain that I wanted help in the way of civilian clothes and information for my potential march to freedom. After a while he understood, but looked definitely hostile, and it became increasingly obvious that any hope of assistance was absolutely.

out of question. He muttered something I could not understand, but I realised that I was jeopardizing my chances of escape by remaining in the house. As I was to learn later, my assumption was correct, for he had sent his

young son to fetch the police. So, smiling pleasantly at my host, I said "Danke" several times and dashed hurriedly through the door, across the yard and back to my old friend the copse.

I was in quite a dilemma now. Should I abandon all thoughts of obtaining help and attempt to gain our lines on my own, or should I try my luck at another farm? I calculated that I was a good week's walking from the front

so I would need food, shelter and some kind of medical assistance. Then, like a light in the dark, came the Intelligence officers tag "Any Dutchman will assist". That decided me. I would try the other farm.

I emerged from the wood again, and this time, almost in darkness, I made towards the second, distant farm. I was unmolested, and in quarter of an hour I was entering the farm-house. The welcome here was entirely different from the last. The old farmer shook me by the hand and led me into the house after ascertaining that nobody had followed me. Before I could speak a word he indicated that I should hide in the nearby barn and return at night when I would get every assistance. I thought this was a grand idea and my

spirits rose accordingly. In the middle of our friendly attempts at conversation the farmer suddenly jumped to his feet, listened for a while and then pushed me into a neighbouring room, closing the door behind me. I was bewildered for a moment, until I heard strange voices in the room I had just left. Then I understood — the enemy were after me again. Time seemed to stand

still as I searched desperately for an exit, but found none. There was no window and the only door was the one leading into the first room. I was forced to wait and hope.

After some minutes the door opened and the friendly farmer appeared with two strange looking men in uniform. They smiled at me and announced briefly in pidgeon English:" Me no German, me Dutch police". I took a deep breath and wondered what would happen next. Would they help me? They were very friendly, sha-

king me by the hand, snapping my back, and handing me cigarettes, but when they told me they would have to hand me over to the Germans, my hopes vanished. They explai= ned that if they did otherwise, they, and their families, would be shot. Since there were two of them, both well armed, I deemed

it judicious to "go quietly".

We walked slowly, as I could hardly move owing to the pain in my rib, and in half an hour we entered the village I had seen

from the wood. I was taken to the police station which occupied quite a prominent po= sition in the centre of the village, and was ushered into the inner office where I was offered a com=

fortable arm-chair, some apples and a glass of milk. These I accepted willingly as I was feeling tired, hungry and thirsty.

One of the policemen went to telephone the German autho= rities to inform them that the hunt was ended and the prey captured.

Another, who spoke a little English, eagerly requested military news. Although I was raging with anger, I explained to him how our forces were pushing forward and liberating Holland while the Dutch were handing me over to the Germans. He sympathized with me, but, nevertheless, my fate was decided.

After half an hour's waiting, a car stopped outside, the door opened, and a group of young German soldiers, armed to the teeth, rushed towards me, completely ignoring the Dutchmen who stood to attention before their masters. I was forced to stand with my hands up while the arrogant young *hooligans* searched me. They completely emptied my pockets, only returning my handkerchief and a couple of apples which the Dutch had given me.

IN GERMAN HANDS

It was quite dark when I left the police station, escorted by the German guards, and climbed into a car which resembled a jeep. I sat in the back with a guard on either side and one in front, while another occupied the seat beside the driver. Their attitude towards me was arrogant, brutal and definitely hostile,

but they refrained from striking me. I realised from their uniforms that they were members of the notorious S.S. division.

After a short drive we arrived in a small blacked-out town and entered the courtyard of a military barracks. I was conducted through the guard-room and down a

long corridor, at the end of which a heavy door was being opened by a guard. Before I knew what was happening, I was pushed into a dark cell and the door was slammed behind me.

I was not left alone for long, however. The door opened, lights were switched on and a crowd of

soldiers in/the blue uniform of the Luftwaffe appeared, led by an officer. I anticipated an interrogation, but was only asked my rank and name by an interpreter. After this they seemed to be rather at a loss as to what they should do next, for they just stood around me in silence. I decided to take the initiative and asked in rather an irritated tone for food, drink and medical aid. The Hauptmann nodded in an almost friendly manner and left, taking with him the rest of the party.

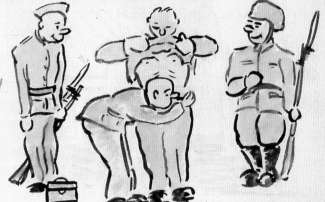

Half an hour went by and the door opened once again. This time a civilian Dutch doctor entered, accompanied by six Germans. He examined my painful ribs and told me, in quite good English, that I had badly bruised and probably cracked them. He then bound me with plaster, shook my hand sympathetically, and took his leave. The Germans, however, remained, and commenced chatting with me in English, and, some who spoke my language, in Polish. Their morale was poor. They seemed depressed about the course of the war, and I did not cheer them any by telling them that they would very soon be either killed or prisoners. After they had brought me some German bread and sausage, a sort of lemonade and two blankets, they left.

I was very tired by now, so, after eating the food, I lay on the hard bench and tried to make myself as comfortable as possible. The hours passed and I was still awake. The pain prevented me from sleeping and my predicament caused me considerable mental anxiety. I felt angry and disappointed, and realising the hopelessness of ~~the~~ my situation ~~in which I was~~, I tried to alleviate the matter by blaming everybody; myself, Dutchmen, police, and, of course, Germans. But one thought was predominant — I could not forget my old squadron flight sergeant, the experienced mechanic, who, two days ago, had volunteered some friendly advice: "Sir", he began, "Your aircraft is due for an inspection which will take two days. I suggest that you have a couple of days rest from ops. You've always flown this aircraft, why take another now?"

Yes, why? How right that old flight sergeant was! In spite of his advice I did not wait for my faithful "A", but took another Mustang with disastrous results.

The explanation was rather a hackneyed one, because so many pilots go missing flying other people's aircraft, that airmen are rather superstitious on that point. I was no exception to the rule. Anyway, it was all over now, and I was about to begin a new chapter in my military career — not a particularly pleasant chapter either.

The events of this exciting day had exhausted me, and I was dead tired, but my mind was still active. I tossed and turned on the uncomfortable wooden bed in an attempt to capture that elusive state — sleep. I relived the details of my capture, and attempts to find some way in which I could elude the arrogant Hun. I still hoped then, that I could find some means to escape.

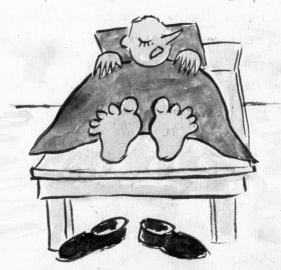

ARNHEIM JAIL

I was rudely awakened early next morning by a German soldier bringing my breakfast which consisted of black bread and black ersatz coffee. I was feeling quite hungry until I tasted the bread, after which I lost my appetite completely.

At first sight, this substance, which is known in Germany as bread, appears to be a sour, unappetising, dark brown mixture. On closer examination one finds that the crusts of the loaf consist almost entirely of sawdust, and the inside is sometimes an under=

cooked, soggy mass, some= times hard and brittle like a dog biscuit. But, whatever consistency the inside, there is always an odour, which does not belie the sour, bitter taste of the bread.

After a short while some guards entered and took me out to a car which was waiting in the court= yard. I climbed in with my escort and soon we were in open country heading, according to the sign-posts I saw, towards Arnheim. We met some German convoys which were coming from the direc= tion of the front and looked in a pretty disordered condition, many vehicles being drawn by horses. We drove through the town of Arnheim and a few miles beyond stopped in front of a building looking unpleasantly like a prison. Sure enough my assumption was correct and a few minutes later

I was incarcerated in a
dismal-looking cell.

Within a few minutes
the door opened to reveal
a Luftwaffe officer who wanted
to know my name, rank and
number. These I gave him, but
when he began asking me
questions about my aircraft
I merely shrugged my shoul-
ders. This brief interrogation
and another search ended the
visit. I spent the remainder
of the day looking through
the window and chewing the
foul German bread given me

by the guard who was a friendly old man, fed up with the war and
the army.

My cell window overlooked a courtyard beyond which I could see
some trees and a road along which numerous Germans were walking.
To see out this window I had to stand on the table as it was very
high up. This was no mean feat for me with my injured rib, nevertheless, I spent the rest of the day with my eyes glued to the bars.

I received only one
blanket in spite of my
frequent requests for
more, and consequently
I was terribly cold
throughout the night. I
spent one of the worst
nights I can remember,
waking up in the mor-
ning with my body

aching all over.

The days passed monotonously, all spent in the same way, until one day, on the 9th September, I think, a youngster in the Dutch Hitler Organisation, who was "Second in Command" of the prison, came to my cell and whispered mysteriously "Kamarad da" and pointed to the next cell. I could get nothing more out of him in spite of my energetic question-

ning. When he left I tapped out "V" on the wall in Morse, and after a while received an answering "V" from the next cell. I went to the window and called out to this "Kamarad" next door and he an-swered me in English with a foreign accent. I immediately became suspicious, thinking that he might be a German whose job it was to get me to talk. After a few minutes, however, I learned that he was a Czech, serving in the R.A.F. and had arrived in the prison the day

ARNHEIM PRISON

Court

Kanewsky

Arct

Stooks

Lavatory

Corridor

Guard Room

Guards

Main Gate

Entrance

before. From that moment on I did not feel so lonely and spent the long hours talking cautiously with my new-found friend.

The next day we were surprised to hear a third voice joining in our conversation. We learned that it belonged to an English flight-lieutenant who was in the cell next door but one to me. So we all stood at our respective windows for the rest of the day, talking and cursing our bad luck.

Occasionally an air raid would relieve the monotony, the Allied aircraft receiving welcoming cheers from us, and a hostile roar from the nearby guns. We all thought that if we were kept in the prison a few days longer we would be liberated by our own troops who should be in the vicinity now.

It was in this prison that I made my first bets on the end of the war. We were all very optimistic, the other two more so than I, so I took both on, the English flight-lieutenant bet that the war would be over by 1st November and the Czech, October. I, of course, won both bets which were for bottles of whisky on return to England.

Thus the days passed slowly, very slowly. I was dirty and unshaven and my tunic was torn from baling out. I was allowed to wash, but the German soap, they gave me, was useless. It was just like a piece of clay and smelled horrible.

I was getting very depressed and wished something would happen, when, at last, on the evening of the 11th the old guard came in and announced "Morgen fruh, raus". I gathered from his gestures that I was to depart from this unfriendly prison.

INTO GERMANY

It was still dark when I was awakened by a body of armed soldiers who rushed into the cell, gave me two minutes in which to dress, and dragged me out. In the corridor I met my two other companions, seeing them for the first time. We were surrounded by guards, armed with all imaginable kinds of weapons — revolvers, rifles, tommy-guns and hand-grenades. There must have been about twenty of them. In the

yard there was a big 'bus confiscated from some Dutch 'bus-company, into which we climbed, three poor, miserable sheep amongst the pack of German wolves.

We went to Arnheim, through streets deserted at this time of the morning, and stopped in front of the railway station. The place was crowded with German Wehrmacht and our guards had some difficulty in finding space in the waiting room. We did not have to wait long. An electric train rolled into the station, we entered one of the empty compartments. By then there were only three of us and three guards, the rest having left us in the station.

After a few hours of uneventful journey we changed on to another train, crowded with Dutch, who looked at us with obvious sympathy, smiling and giving "V" signs. Round about lunch time we reached Venlo, still in Holland, and left the train. We marched along the streets to a large building, occupied by Luftwaffe, where we had a few hours rest, some vegetable soup and sat on the bench, prohibited to talk and guarded by a German with tommy-gun in his hands. We could only look at each other and whisper an odd sentence when the guard was not looking. Then we were off again, we marched back to the station, with three new guards, some of whose belongings we had to carry in spite of our protests.

We had a rather unpleasant time at the station, whilst waiting for a train. A huge crowd of Hitlerjugend approached, led by a most arrogant-looking officer, a youngster of about 17.

They surrounded us, laughing, spitting and making rude remarks about us. But for our guards we would probably have had a pretty rough time at the hands of these hoobjans. Fortunately the train arrived and we were once again seated in a compartment especially emptied for us.

I cannot remember how many times we changed trains, but the whole journey was like a night-mare. Sometimes we had to wait for hours on the stations, sometimes the train would stop in the open country, probably because of an air-raid, sometimes we moved slower than walking pace.

I remember, though, when we crossed the German border, because my spirits sank. While still in Holland, I was hoping to escape, in Germany my chances were almost nil.

The next morning saw us still in the train, slowly moving in south= =easterly direction.

Our few meals consisted of black bread and, occasionaly, a cup of coffee in German Red Cross canteens.

Later in the morning we saw an air raid by lots of Flying Fortresses, flak and bombs rained down on one of the towns we had just left. This raid caused an enormous confusion in the railway system

and we only reached Frankfurt on Main at 11 o'clock in the morning.

Here our real troubles commenced. The town had been raided at night by the R.A.F., debris was still smoking, and the station was crowded with refugees, who, of course, were not very friendly towards us. As soon

as we stepped out of the station, an old "gentleman" rushed towards us with a stick, raised to hit us, some women spat aggresively and some workers rushed towards us with hostile shouts. Our guards decided to return to the station and, after a conference with the station master, we boarded another train. Alighting at a small station nearby, we started walking towards the prisoners camp.

avoiding the town. We walked for about an hour before we reached the suburbs of Frankfurt from opposite direction. Then, suddenly,

a German worker appeared, glared at us and pulled out a great revolver with obvious intentions. Two of our guards intervened, fighting the infuriated man, while we retreated with the third guard.

Our next trouble was to come a few minutes later. Some German soldiers, driving in a car, suddenly swerved and careered straight towards us. We jumped

out of the way to avoid being run over, but the mudguard caught me and sent me spinning. Fortunately, I only suffered minor bruises.

Arriving at the tram depot we had to wait some time, while a crowd of Germans glared at us, jabbering

something which was unintelligable but sounded anta=
gonistic. It was very exciting, but I and my companions
were of the opi=
nion that we had
had enough exci=
tement to last
us for some ti=
me. Consequently,
we were greatly
relieved when
the tram arrived
and we comple=
ted our journey

without further incident. We left the tram and, after a
short walk, entered the gates of Oberürsel Interrogation
Prison Camp.

OBERÜRSEL

At the foot of a delightful wooded hillside nestled the Interrogation Camp, consisting of some six or seven buildings, above which numerous model farms were built among the trees. The picturesque scene was further enhanced by an old church, its tower protruding from the woods. A short walk along the charming bridle-path brought one to the top of the hill, from where one could see Frankfurt on the right and Bad Homburg on the left. This then was the setting in which I found myself at 13.00 hours of 12th September. We were ushered into a large, bare room, segregated and forced to strip completely, while the Germans thoroughly searched our clothing, even socks and shoes. When the search was over, we were allowed to dress, and then locked into different cells, losing touch with each other for the time being.

I had requested medical attention and, shortly after entering my cell, a German doctor arrived, examined my ribs, changed the plaster and assured me that the injury was not

serious. It might
not be serious, but
it was certainly
painful!

I expected to
be interrogated soon
after arriving, but
nothing happened
and I spent the
day on the hard,
slatted bed, on which
lay a sack filled
with wood shavings,

shivering with cold and just meditating. Each time I wished to obey
the call of nature I had to signal the guard by twisting a knob
on the wall by the door. This product of the inventive German

mind was a strip atta-
ched to the wall
outside, and connec-
ted to the knob in-
side. When the knob
was turned, the
strip was allowed
to drop and clatter,
thus arousing the
attention of the
guard, who would
open the cell, if
he felt so.inclined.

Meals consisted
of the notorious black
bread, two slices for
breakfast and two

for tea. For lunch there was a plate of very watery soup. With the bread we had a cup of German coffee, or, a concotion which the guards proclaimed as "Das Thee". This so-called tea was not a bit like our conception of the delectable beverage. It smelled very strongly of herbs, had an indescribable taste and a yellowish colour.

When the food was issued, each cell was unlocked and the inmate stood in the doorway to receive the meagre rations. It was while waiting my turn that I noticed my neighbour in "8B", I myself being in "10 B". He was a tall, red headed squadron leader in a dirty R.A.F. battle dress, his face adorned by an enormous flowing moustache. Whenever tea or coffee was issued, he produced a large wine bottle, which the Germans always had difficulty in filling. This was Geoff Rothwell, who was later to become my companion and best friend in my prison life.

The next day my cell was opened and I was escorted along the corridors by a guard.

I thought this must be the interrogation and nerved myself for the battle of wits which would ensue. I was wrong, however, because I was taken into a room where an N.C.O. with a Leica camera took my photograph while a board with

my service number on was hung around my neck. The operation lasted for a few minutes, then I was taken back to my cell. Later on I had an opportunity to see these photographs which were awful.

The days dragged even more so than when I was in Arnheim jail and I grew more and more furious that an officer should be treated in such a manner. Eventually, after four days, the guard entered, pushed me out of the cell and took me along the corridors, through the yard outside and into a block of German offices. I was shown into one of the numerous rooms, where, behind the desk littered with papers, sat an elderly German corporal. This was to be my interrogator.

He arose, smiling pleasantly, and shook my hand cordially. He then,

apologised for the awful conditions I was living in, and promised to arrange for my transfer to a proper prisoners of war camp as soon as possible. After offering me a chair, he

produced a case and gave me a Turkish cigarette, which I gratefully accepted, not having seen one of any sort for days.

He had a sheet of paper on the desk in front of him and after consulting it for some minutes, asked me to confirm my name, rank, number and locality in which I landed. I complied, surprised that he did not ask any further questions but just chatted amiably about the war and the Allied offensive, giving me the latest news. He kept offering me cigarettes which I accepted, and promised to arrange for me to have a shower, shave and use of the library. Thus ended my first interrogation, leaving me very bewildered as I returned to my cell.

I thoroughly enjoyed my shower and shave, and left the washroom feeling a very different man after ridding myself of a beard an inch long. I spent the remainder of the day reading a book about Alpine climbing, which I drew from the small library.

I expected to leave this depressing camp in the near future, but I found myself in the same cell, in the same corridor, in the same camp, four days later when once again I was sent for by my interrogator. This time he talked mainly about himself only mentioning the R.A.F. and its activities very

occasionally. I just listened and sometimes
nodded, not wishing to
take part in conversa-
tion in case he caught
me out.

In the afternoon
he took me for a walk
after had given my pa-
role. I was rather dubious
about giving parole, but
after consideration I de-
cided for it. It was
valid for one day only

and I badly needed fresh air and exercise. We walked through
the beautiful woods surrounding Oberürsel, stopping at a small
Gesthaus. Our conversation was about the end of the war,
and I almost convinced him that in a few months time he
would be an Allied P.O.W., and Germany conquered. He told

me he would try
his outmost to ha-
ve me transferred
to a permanent
camp.

Nevertheless,
I spent twelve
days altogether in
my solitary cell
before I was trans-
sterred. Before
leaving I had a
final interrogation
during which I was

offered some French vin ordinaire, sardine sandwiches and a packed of cigarettes. So, taking all in all, my interrogator did not treat me so badly, compared with the guards, who were rude and arrogant. How-ever, I learnt la-ter, that he had known a great deal about me, and my treatment must have been some strange sort of policy.

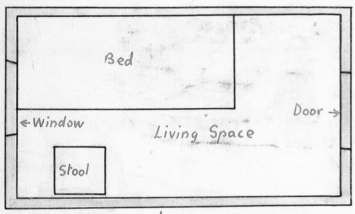

On the eve-ning of 23rd September I was transferred to a barracks where there were about fifty men of different rank and nationality. There were American aircrew, R.A.F. aircrew, R.A.F. Regiment personnel and paratroopers captured at Arnheim. We were accomodated in small rooms, twelve in each of them and spent a very uncomfortable night there.

Before we could go to sleep, we were assembled outside the barracks where we were informed that we were expected to "behave like officers and N.C.O.'s that we were, and like gentlemen which we were supposed to be." We had to give our parole not to escape during the journey,

otherwise we would be deprived of our shoes, belts and braces and put under a double guard. Then we were allowed to go to sleep.

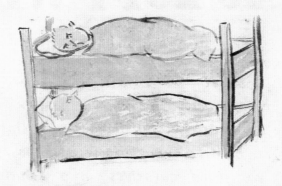

DULAG LUFT WETZLAR

Early next morning we were assembled again, some eighty of us, outside the barracks and were marched to the station. As there was not a great number of people about at the time, we arrived at the railway station unmolested by anyone. We had to wait about two hours for a train and finally we found ourselves in a compartment carefully guarded.

The journey was long and uneventful. We received no food, and everyone longed for a cigarette. A few of us had cigarettes of some kind and were watched enviously by the less fortunate ones.

I MUST APOLOGISE FOR THE INACCURACY OF THE SKETCH ON THE LEFT. THE KRIEGIES ARE SHOWN CARRYING KIT BAGS, WHILE IN ACTUAL FACT, WE HAD NO LUGGAGE ON ARRIVAL AT DULAG LUFT, BUT WERE EQUIPPED THERE.

THE DISTURBING INFLUENCE OF GOONS AROUND THE BARRACKS WHILE I WAS WORKING, IS RESPONSIBLE FOR THE ERROR.

Late in the afternoon we arri‐ ved at Wetzlar station, left the train and marched through the little town and out into the country towards the Dulag Luft Transit Camp.

This camp was built on similar lines to the permanent pri‐ soner camp in Germany. Part of it was surrounded by a doub‐ le row of high barbed wire fence with four watch towers on the corners, where a German guard with machine-gun watched the prisoners. The other part of the camp, where we were ta‐ ken, was occupied by German offi‐ ces and quarters.

Of course, there was a tho‐ rough search, though it is difficult to

conceive how we could acquire any weapon or escape kit since the last search. Then they checked our papers and took

us over to the proper camp, where we were given showers and shown to a wooden barracks, that was to be our home for the next week.

It was in this camp that I first saw the Red Cross food. There was a communal mess hall with about twelve tables, each seating 14 men. The food was brought in and placed at the end of the table by British and American N.C.O's. On American tables it was

rather a case of grab-what-you--can and those nearest the food usually had the largest helpings. Our first meal was a mixture of salmon and potatoes, cheese and biscuits. It tasted wanderful after Oberürsel diet.

Our room was a small one and into it were packed

like sardines 20 officers and N.C.O's, sleeping on three--tier metal bunks. When we arrived, we were issued with kit-bags containing soap, razor, vest, pants, cigarettes, razor blades, sewing-kit and other odd items which were invaluable in prison life.

There were five squadron leaders in our group and it was not long before we became acquainted and stuck together during our stay in Dulag Luft. The American colonel, who was in charge of the P's o.W. in the camp used to call us "The five sad sack squadron leaders". The reason for and meaning of this strange expression was rather obscure.

There were two roll calls each day, when we were counted and a fat German major appeared from the direction of the

COME ON, YOU FIVE SAD SACK SQUADRON LEADERS!

USA

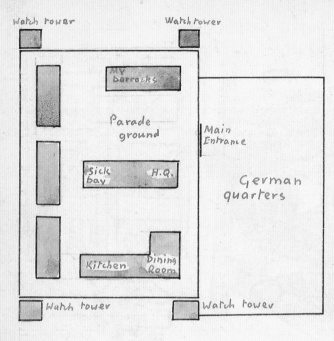

Watch tower Watch tower

MV barracks

Parade ground

Main Entrance

German quarters

Sick bay H.Q.

Kitchen Dining Room

Watch tower Watch tower

offices and requested the colonel to dismiss us. We had numerous air raids, when we were hurried into shelters which were always overcrowded. Those standing in the entrance were constantly endangered to a risk of being shot by the guards walking outside and watching that no prisoner would show his head outside the shelter. Somehow we managed to see the large formations of Flying Fortresses accompanied by Thunderbolts and always cheered them loudly as they were passing by.

There was not much to do in this camp and we all wanted to go as soon as possible and find at last our permanent camp, where we could settle down a bit.

Nevertheless I had to wait six days before I saw my name on the board outside the mess-hall. There was a large group of officers going to a camp called Stalag Luft 1 in Barth and I was one of them. So I spent the last night in Wetzlar and had a chance to watch some of my fellow prisoners, officers, as they were equipped with great broomes and ordered to clean the lavatory. Fortunately I missed that "pleasure".

PER ARDUA AD BARTH

Next morning we were all assembled, counted by the Germans and after another search we set off in a long column, surrounded by swarms of armed soldiers. We walked back to the town of Wetzlar, passed the streets crowded by people watching us curiously, and we headed towards the railway station, right in the middle of the town.

As we entered the station I became rest= less, anticipating the possibility of escaping, but, unfortu= nately, there was none. The Germans would take no risks and guarded us cautiously all the time. We were taken

to the goods yard where two large wagons waited for us, with the heavily barred windows. We recei= ved half a Red Cross parcel each and were shown inside, taking places in com= partments, ten of us in each. It was uncom= fortable right from the beginning and by the end

of the journey it became almost unbearable.

Our wa= gons were con= nected with a train and in the afternoon we star= ted off. The vo= yage lasted four days and four nights, during which we had to remain in the overcrowded compartments. Our food consisted of Red Cross parcels and the issue of Ger= man bread. Occasionally we would get a cup of black coffee, but never had any hot meal. Consequently all kinds of stomach trouble soon started among us, and, having only one toilet per wagon, we had to form long queues, comparing with which the house= wifes queues in En= gland would seem ridiculously short and pleasant entertainment. Of course there was no water for washing or shaving and we looked extremely dirty, like a bunch of tramps. At nights we suffered from severe cold, shi= vering and dreaming

about overcoats and blankets, which existed only in our
dreams.

   We travelled right across Germany, stopping
at many stations and waiting often several hours in open
fields. Eventually we approached Berlin, passed through its
suburbs and had a chance to take a glance at the ruined
houses and factories. Then we turned north, and on the
fourth day in the afternoon, hungry and exhausted we
alighted at the small desolate railway station of Barth,

the famous "Barth on the Baltic". That was our terminus, the rest of the journey we had to make on foot.

STALAG LUFT 1 BARTH

We set off in column towards our destination, escorted by well armed guards, some leading unpleasant looking hounds. In half an hour time we were passing through the gates of the camp which were covered with barbed wire. It was rather depressing, as the place looked extremely well guarded, with double barbed wire fences and numberless watch towers equipped with machine guns. We were all shown to a wooden barrack, where

we were segregated; stripped once again and searched. Then our identity was checked and we were taken to a small brick building, where we were deloused, checked over by a British doctor, and then enjoyed a long, hot shower, which we needed so badly after four days journey in the train. Next

we went to the clothing
stores, were equipped with
some shirts, blankets, mattress
covers, boots and a few more
items, all clothing of British
or American origine, and
finally we went to the pro=
per camp, separated by a
fence, where, at last, we
got rid of our guards and
where a British officer took care of us.

On that side of the camp I was loudly cheered by
a group of kriegies / that was a popular name for P.o.W./, I re=
cognised some of my friends who had been shot down a few

months before my unfortuna=
te visit to Goonland took
place. I could hardly recog=
nise Jan Pentz, whom I had
known very well in England,
because of his great mou=
stache, an enormous effort,
covering almost half of his
face. I had to tell those
people my story and all the latest news and rumours.
Of course, their first question was "When will the war
end" and to that I
answered "In a few
months". Well, I was
quite convinced my=
self that it would
be over by Christ=
mas 1944.

I was then showed to my future "home", barracks No 11. It was not a very luxurious place, I would rather say it was awful. Cold, overcrowded and with no indoor conveniences, it had to accommodate sixteen people in one room the size of medium bed room. We had double bunks instead of beds and wooden boards instead of springs.

Fortunately three of us, Geoff, "Woody" and I, all squadron leaders, were accommodated in a tiny room by the end of the barrack, and though we had very little space, we had some privacy, which in prison camp is a precious thing.

The whole camp, containing about nine thousand

prisoners, was divided into several compounds, called in German "Lagers", our being the main one. Fourteen habitable barracks were crowded there. On one end of the compound there was a huge barrack for kitchen, church and theatre, the

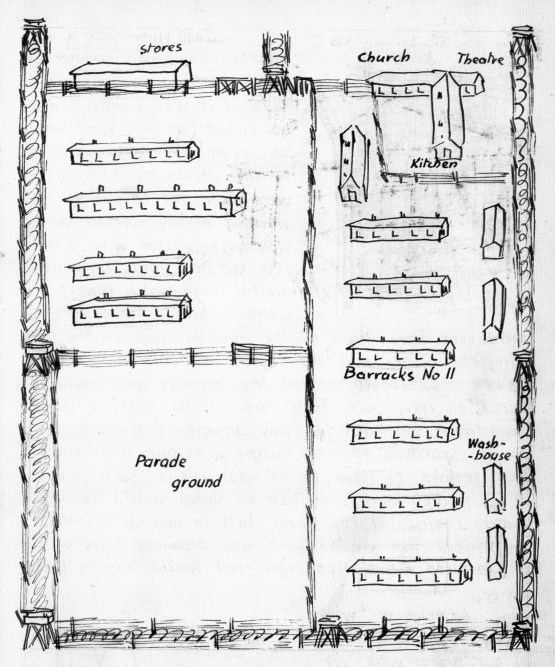

latter built and equiped entirely by prisoners. On the
other end we had parade grounds, where all the roll
calls used to take place, and where in our spare
time we could play soccer, rugger, soft ball and several
other British and American games.

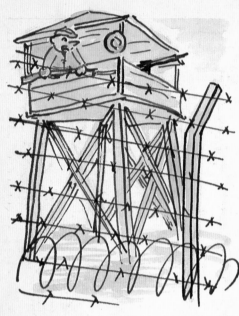

The camp was heavily guarded by double barbed wire fence. Some ten yards inside of it was another fence, so called "warning wire", which was prohibited to be crossed by the prisoners. The guards were instructed to fire without warning at any person who would cross that wire. Every few hundred yards there were erected high watch towers. German guards seemed to be everywhere. They stood by the machine guns in the towers, continously patrolled inside and outside the camp, walked and stooged around the barracks and could be found at every gate. They had special party, a search department, who used to pay unexpected visits to the rooms, searching for the escape aids and any weapon that seemed to them to be dangerous. Such things as a pocket knife, iron bar or shovel would be immediately confiscated, the same fate to any clothes that might look like civilian suit, any drawings, diary or unpunctured tin of Red Cross food would also be taken away.

Although we were in captivity and deprived of our proper work, we had rather a busy time. We had to do all the work ourselves, so from early morning until late evening we would do the hard house-wife's jobs.

I learnt how to make fire in the morning, using only some waste paper and card boards to eco= nomise in coal, and how to boil the water on that meagre fire. I learnt the necessity of running a few hundred yards to the outdoor wash-house to have a wash in icy cold water. I also learnt

how to use some other, very primitive place, which was standing good three hundred yards from the bar=

racks, no indoor conven= iences being available. These jobs would start the normal day and routine work.

The first morning bugle would be sounded fifteen minutes before the roll call, followed by another one, five minutes before the ceremony. Everybody would be ordered to the pa=

rade ground where we would fall into the respec= tive "squadrons". All the sick cases and people unable to walk were permitted to remain in the barracks and would be counted sepa=

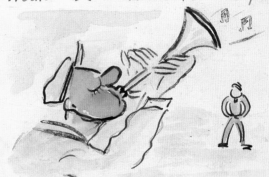

rately. It usually took about half an hour for the Germans to count us, unless they made a miscount, in which case the whole ceremony would have to be

repeated. These miscounts used to happen quite often, the Germans being obviously not too strong in arytmethics, and would cause a great deal of anger among the prisoners, who had to wait long time, often without the breakfast. Then, we would be re= leased and could do what we wished, until the next, afternoon roll call.

Of course, after the roll call we could find our bar= rack locked and a crowd of ugly looking Germans searching inside and turning out all our belongings. These searches lasted several hours and we never knew when to expect them and what would be confiscated. Fortunately, during my stay in Stalag Luft I I had only two searches in my room,

and somehow they never took anything
from me, although once I had a narrow
escape with this log-book.

    Quite naturally we were all
very eager for news from the outside
world, especially the war news. We were
officially allowed to listen to the German wireless, which was installed in
some of the barracks, we were also
receiving the German propaganda news-
papers in English. Of course, that propa-

ganda business had very little
effect on us, we were taking
it humorously, as it was rather
funny to hear or read that
Hitler was an ingenious angel
and the Germans harmless sheep,
betrayed and forced to the war
by the other bloodthirsty nations.

The German communiquee was regularly translated and put
on the black-board outside the Barracks 5, in which we
had our office and where the Senior British Officer lived. In
the same barracks there was a large wall-map with the
both fronts marked and as the
war situation changed, the lines
on the map would be moved
accordingly.

    Every morning Geoff
and I used to take long walks
around the compound, as we
always felt the necessity of
physical exercise. These walks
became a great attraction to us,

as we could then talk freely about our experiences during the war, about our remote homes and the people we left

there. We would meet a lot of other Kriegies also promenading, because almost everybody needed the fresh air and a bit of free= dom. The path around the camp was always crowded with pri= soners, pacing the hard ground and deep in their thoughts or talks with their friends and room-mates.

Still, we could not enjoy it for long time. As I said before, we had to prepa= re our own meals and look after ourselves, and all the food was issued to us before lunch. Thus we had to collect boxes, buckets and bowls and queue in the kitchen or other places, sometimes quite

distant from our barracks. It was hard work, we had to distribute and divide various products, we had to carry bowls of barley, potatoes, swe= des, Red Cross parcels, coal, hot water, bread, soup and all kinds of other items. Then, after we had placed them safely into our impro=

vised cupboard, we would get cracking on the lunch, ta= king that duty in turns, ex= perimenting and proving our cooking abilities, recollecting the meals we used to have at ho= me and often inventing delicious "special kriegie's" dishes.

After lunch we were always enjoying the other kind of news, the good old BBC. There was a wireless set hidden cleverly somewhere in the camp in one of the barracks. Of course it was strictly prohibited and the Germans, knowing about the secret radio, were continuously searching, getting gradually mad with

rage, but they were never able to trace it. They kept searching for hours, turning the barracks "upside down", all in vain. It

was quite an organisation: access to the actual set was only allowed to a few people, but the BBC communiquees were typed and delivered to special "news offi-

cers who circulated the news inside the barracks. To avoid being caught by the Germans, we had established a duty of "Goon Guard". The word Goon stood for German. I still don't know how it was originated. Anyhow there were Goon Guards standing by entrances to every barracks and as soon as any German approached, our guard would shout aloud "Enemy up". At this sign all illegal activity would cease, the news sheet would be smartly hidden in somebody's pocket, and the Germans never knew what was going on before their arrival. Thus we were always up to date with the latest events, having a clear picture of the war happenings.

There is a lot to say about trading in the camp. There were two kinds. First, we used to trade among ourselves, mostly for food, cigarettes and chocolate, and having no money, we created another currency — cigarettes! Therefore a bar of chocolate would reach the value of 200 cigarettes, tin of margarine would equal half a tin of bully beef and so on. The other kind of trading was exchange of goods with the Germans. They were in desperate need of cigarettes and coffee, we knew that and had plenty of both. So we could obtain from them all sorts of things, which they would bring in secrecy, as they were strictly prohibited to trade with us.

From dusk till dawn we had to remain inside the barracks, the door and windows were locked and prisoners would be shot if they attempted to go out. Through the holes in the walls one could see the empty camp, strong lamps illuminating the barbed wire and beams of searchlights moving slowly to and fro. Guards with dogs

were wandering inside the compounds, several patrols circulated outside. There was absolutely no chance of slipping through that net.

The time went by, weeks and months passed since my arrival in Stalag, and I steadily accustomed myself to the new conditions of life. It was not easy and required a great deal of will power to master the sudden spells of depression. The winter came and we suffered from intense cold, the climate being severe in that part of Germany. We had no warm coats and in addition the barracks proved to be very draughty, and the small issue of coal entirely insufficient. We used to stay in our tiny room, shivering around the iron stove and putting on all clothes available. Going to bed we would dress instead of undress and still we would wake up in the morning stiff with the cold.

THE STARVATION PERIOD

In January 1945 Geoff and I were transferred to another barrack, No 5, much more comfortable, as it had been built a few years ago. The barrack was more

solid, warmer and had the indoor conveniences. From then we lived in larger room, six of us together. But the real trouble was about to begin. The Red Cross parcels, our main food, were coming in shorter and shorter supply, and by the beginning of February they ceased to arrive, leaving us entirely on German rations. Well, the characteristic point was, that these rations were not big enough to live on, and too big to die.

We had to satisfy our stomachs with black bread, potatoes and swedes, and even those items were scarce. Hunger and shortly after starvation commenced. Our daily diet consisted then of four thin slices

of black bread, one or two potatoes per head, the same amount of swedes, the latter being so tasteless that a respectable cow would refuse to consume them, a little bit of margarine and three or four cups of German coffee. We used to divide the incoming rations cautiously, under the strict control of all the inhabitants of our room, watching that the portions were evenly cut. Our topic of conversation became food, and we used to compose and discuss the non-existent menues, which we would consume...one day.

We were getting thinner and thinner, our reserve of fat disappearing rapidly, we would feel cold more intensely and had a continous feeling of hunger and pain inside. Every physical effort would cost us a lot of energy, we cut down our walking and playing games, most of the time lying on our bunks, reading books and... talking about food. The rumours spread fantastically. People were talking of thousands of Red Cross parcels on the way, they would say that a friend of somebody's friend actually saw the trucks loaded with food coming to the camp, but, inevitably, it would prove a pure rumour, we were still on swede-potato diet.

The Spring was here, warm and beautiful Spring, for days

ANY GEN?!

no cloud could be seen on the blue sky. We all longed for fresh air, but our weakness prevented us from
exercises. Only very courageous and the strongest of
us risked walking and occasionally playing games,
especially the volley-ball, which was our favourite
sport. We had a court just outside our barracks, and

used to play the ga-
me, until some of
the players felt too
hungry and exhau-
sted to continue.
We had to lie down
for hours after the
game to recover
and regain the strenght.

Other games, American soft ball, soccer and rugger were
played very seldom now, and their tempo slowed down
considerably, people being often unable to run and kick
the ball properly. It was a pitiful sight to watch the
soccer, which used to be on a very high standard before the hunger period. Players would "crawl" on the
field, being exhausted after first five minutes of the
game, but still not
giving up, and con-
tinuing their efforts.
     The main
attraction was then
the camp theatre,
it did not require
any effort to sit
down in an arm=
chair, constructed
cleverly from empty

Red Cross boxes. We had really excellent artists, managers and decorators, often professional, and the plays were on a high level. We had every kind of shows, from the revue, through the light comedy to the drama. There was also a camp orchestra, consisting of some fourty musicians, the instruments kindly delivered by the marvellous International Red Cross Society. We were able to enjoy listening

to Chopin, Grieg, Tschaikovsky or Bethoven, these entertainments allowing us to have some relaxation and forget for a while the awful food problem. Still, the show would come to an end, we would have to stagger back to our room, and the old trouble would start again. You cannot cheat a stomach which is hopelessly empty.

WE MAY GET FOUR SLICES EACH...

As a special treat we used to prepare an extra "brew", a cup of watery German coffee without sugar. In March we were deprived even that beverige of doubtful value. The Germans ran out of coffee supply and produced that horrid concoction, which they dared to call tea. It always reminded

me of the herbs to cure kidney trouble.

Then, by the end of March, a strong rumour spread, that there were thirty thousand Red Cross parcels arriving in the camp. The rumour repeated for several days, but, of course, we would not believe it, having several false alarms before. The pesimists said that somebody misunderstood the news and these were thirty thousand razor blades coming, few "optimists" insisted that the parcels arrived, but contained sport articles.

However, this time the rumour proved to be the truth! The parcels were here, loads of them. Big trucks were coming daily and soon we knew that they would last us till the end of the war, and that all our food troubles ended.

People went mad with eating and arranging the innumerous "glutton parties". There was abundance of food now, no need to economise, and we all commenced to introduce to life those elaborate menues we had invented and dreamed about during the starvation period.

It so happened that the Red Cross parcels we should have received, had been wrongly directed by the German authorities to some other place, and, only after those long months the Goons realised their mistake and corrected the fault. This was the reason for all our sufferings.

Anybow we were able now to produce an imposing meal, a real treat for Easter dinner. We spent almost three hours consuming it, and by the end of the meal we all felt very satisfied, but a bit sick. Easter proved to be a real eating holiday in our camp.

5 MINUTES TO TWELVE

Since the beginning of April there was a wave of optimism and tension in the camp. The front lines were so deep inside Germany that some of the more optimistic Kriegies started packing their belongings, expecting to go home any day. The news-board was continually besieged by

a great crowd of prisoners, hungry for sensational news. The Goons, those who understood English, gazed stupidly at the board, commenting grimly the communiquees of the German High Command, who could not hide any more the grave situation in which the Reich was. There was no doubt to any thinking person, that the German State was cracking and that the final stage of the war was approaching at a big pace.

Meantime the life in the camp was going seemingly as usual, we still were busy cooking and doing our "housewife's" jobs, but nobody could raise any enthusiasm and be really interested in that boring work. The weather was perfect, we used to lie down outside the barracks, sunbathing and talking about the near liberation.

The bets on the approaching date of D-day were very common, all kinds of rumours spread among the excited people. Very often the Germans would spread them, their spirits sunken so low that they almost felt our prisoners and were asking for our protection when the time will come. One day the rumour went that it was Montgomery's army spearheads that were seen fifty miles from us and were pushing towards us, another day the

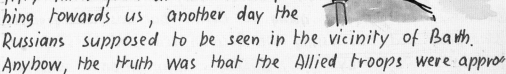

Russians supposed to be seen in the vicinity of Barth. Anybow, the truth was that the Allied troops were approaching us from both sides, the distance from them growing smaller and smaller. It looked like a sort of race between the British and Russians, our place being the objectif, and we were betting who would reach us first.

Some of our guards were posted to the front lines to defend their collapsing Vaterland, they were going reluctantly and showing no fighting spirit. To replace them we enjoyed the arrival of the Volksturm, the last German hope, a bunch of old men, who could hardly walk and were probably the veterans of the 1871 war. These

men were thoroughly fed up with the war and the disaster Hitler brought to Germany, but they still had to obey orders and guarded us cautiously. However, nobody would try to escape at this stage and we were sure that the next few weeks would decide our fate.

The air raids occured very often, we could see not only the bombers going to Berlin, but also the fighters, sweeping and harrassing the German rear and lines of communication. It was certainly most encouraging sight, as it indicated the approachment of our troops.

By the end of April the tension came to a climax. British troops crossed the Elbe, the Russians broke through and were fanning across the Oder, they were just about to join up. We seemed to be in the pocket of German resistance, if that haphasard fighting and mass surrender could be called "ressistance". Talks started about the evacuation, the Goons obviously preparing to leave the camp, as they feared the Russians more than enybody else. Every morning we looked through the window, glancing at the nearest watch tower, to see whether the guards were still there, we anticipated their flight during the night. We could clearly hear the distant guns, roaring nearer and nearer, and developping into a continous thunder.

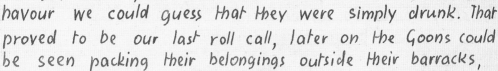

Then came the greatest day in our prison life. In the afternoon on 30st of April, we noticed during the roll call that the Germans were strangely excited, and from their be-havour we could guess that they were simply drunk. That proved to be our last roll call, later on the Goons could be seen packing their belongings outside their barracks,

there was no question, they were going. They did not appear to lock the gates and the barracks, after the dusk they fled silently, lea-ving us in charge of the camp. We were well prepa-red for that eventuality. Orders were issued, we produced our own guards, or rather the Military Police, outside the Commandant's office we put a big white flag, pat-rols were sent to get in touch with the ap-proaching Russians. At last we were free.

We woke up on the 1st of May with a strange feeling of freedom. There were no Goons around,

we were all very relieved and eagerly awaited for the arrival of the first Allied troops. By the evening one of our patrols returned, accompanied by some Russian officers. Soon the three flags, Russian, British and American were erected on the mast, we were liberated.

Another week passed and our evacuation to the British lines was arranged, we left the unpleasant camp and after a few hours' journey found ourselves among our army. Two days later we landed in England, which ended my Kriegie's experiences, and at that moment my story comes to an end.

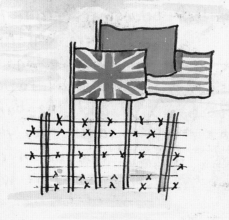

WESTERN FRONT SEPTEMBER 1944

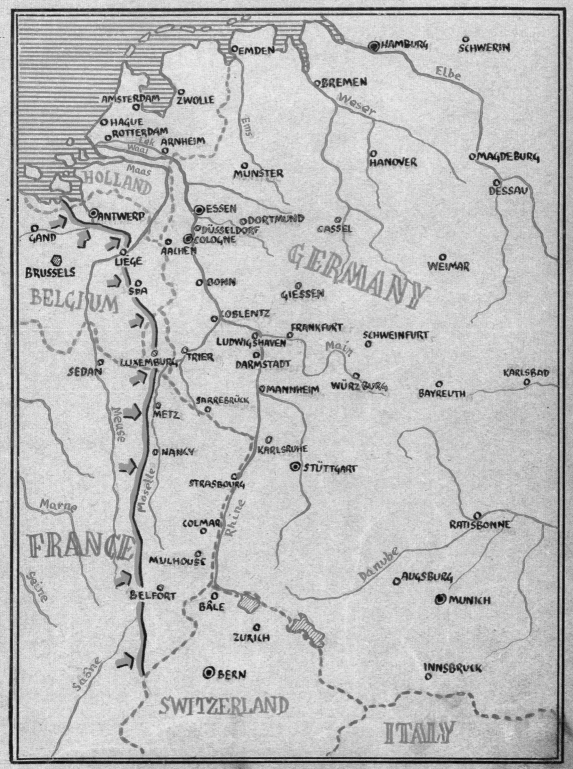

GERMAN OFFENSIVE DECEMBER 44

RUSSIAN OFFENSIVE JANUARY 1945

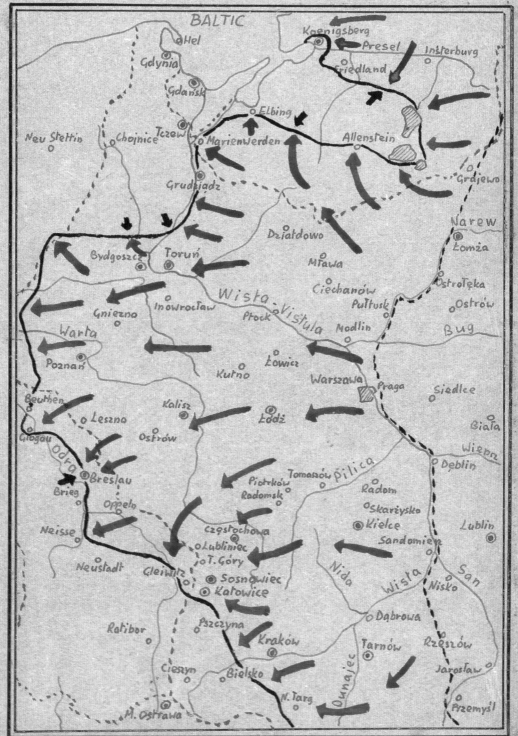

EUROPEAN FRONTS 1ST FEBRUARY

EUROPEAN FRONTS 1ST MARCH 1945

EUROPEAN FRONTS 1ST APRIL 1945

EUROPEAN FRONTS 1ˢᵗ MAY 1945

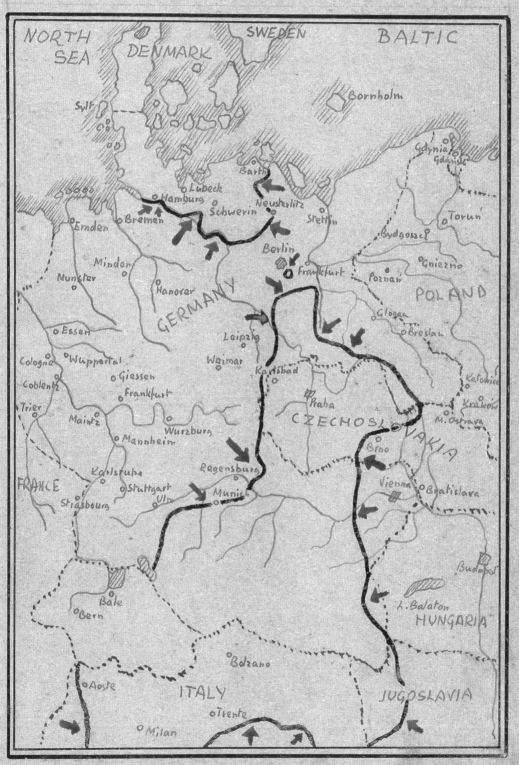

an american
RED CROSS PARCEL

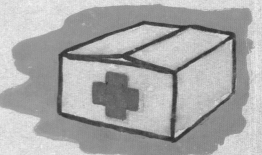

1 lb **SPAM**

1 lb **CORNED BEEF**

1 lb **POWDERED MILK**

1 lb **MARGARINE**

½ lb **CHEESE**

½ lb **SALMON**

½ lb **SUGAR**

1 lb **CHOCOLATE**

1 lb **RAISINS OR PRUNES**

½ lb **JAM**

CONTAINS

12 **BISCUITS**

100 **CIGARETTES**

6 oz **LIVER PATÉ**

2 oz **COFFÉE**

2 BARS **SOAP**

1 oz **SALT & PEPPER**

12 **VITAMIN PILLS**

RED CROSS PARCEL

a british

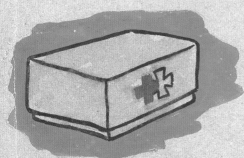

CONTAINS

1 lb
BEEF OR STEW

1/2 lb
MEAT ROLL

1/2 lb
SALMON

1 lb
VEGETABLES

6 oz
CHEESE

1 lb
JAM

1 lb
CONDENSED MILK

4 oz
SUGAR

1 lb
SAUSAGES

1/2 lb
BACON

1/2 lb
CHOCOLATE

1/2 lb
PRUNES OR APRICOTS

2 oz
COCOA

1 BAR
SOAP

12
BISCUITS

4 oz
POWDERED EGGS

2 oz
PORRIDGE

1 oz
TEA

50
CIGARETTES

12
VITAMIN PILLS

GERMAN RATIONS

WEEKLY	GRAMMES	
	OLD RATE	W.E.F. 26·2·45
MARGARINE	150	100
BLACK BREAD	1960	1800
FAT	42	18
CHEESE	27	25
POTATOES	3290	3360
DRIED VEGETABLES	70	48
SUGAR	155	140
JAM	155	110
SAUSAGE	100	110
BARLEY	57	45

FOOD

OCTOBER

OTHER ITEMS

MARGE

VEG

POTATOES

BREAD

RED CROSS PARCELS

NOVEMBER

OTHER ITEMS

MARGE

VEG

POTATOES

BREAD

RED CROSS PARCELS

DECEMBER

OTHER ITEMS

MARGE

VEG

POTATOES

BREAD

RED CROSS PARCELS

JANUARY

OTHER ITEMS

MARGE

VEG

POTATOES

BREAD

RED CROSS PARCELS

PROBLEM

FEBRUARY

OTHER ITEMS   MARGE   VEG   POTATOES   BREAD   RED CROSS PARCELS

MARCH

1/2

OTHER ITEMS   MARGE   VEG   POTATOES   BREAD   RED CROSS PARCELS

APRIL

OTHER ITEMS   MARGE   VEG   POTATOES   BREAD   RED CROSS PARCELS

MAY

HOME

OTHER ITEMS   MARGE   VEG   POTATOES   BREAD   RED CROSS PARCELS

1944

THE WINGLESS LUFTWAFFE

GERMANY'S LATEST WEAPON

1945

V29

VOLKSTURM IN ACTION

MOST SECRET

To: ~ ~ ~ *HAUPTBUHMAN*   A. Nr. *6343/*

                                          L. Nr. *144*

NOTICE

The watch found amongst your belongings is property of the   **British Air Ministry**
                                                                U. S. Army A. C.

and has therefore been confiscated according to War regulations.

Watch Nr.:   *A. M. 6B/234*

Auswertestelle West,   *den 14/9 44*   *[signature]*

5510/44 Heidelberger Gutenberg-Druckerei GmbH. IX. 44.

"DER TERRORFLIEGER"

Name:	A R C T
Vorname:	Bohdan
Dienstgrad:	S/Ldr. Major
Erk.-Marke:	5849
Serv.-Nr.:	P-1090
Nationalität:	britisch, Pole

Baracke: 6

Raum: 2

K. Liebig-Sagan

This particular document, my "Identity Card" in Stalag Luft, was made after my arrival here, and discovered after the liberation of our camp.

CAMP CURRENCY

CHOCOLATE RATION BAR

4 OUNCES NET

INGREDIENTS: Sugar, Chocolate, Skim Milk Powder, Cocoa Fat, Artificial Flavoring, 0.450 mg. Vitamin B_1 (Thiamin Hydrochloride). and Oat Flour.

Packed by

WALTER BAKER AND COMPANY, INC.

Dorchester, Mass.

Chesterfield CIGARETTES

LIGGETT & MYERS TOBACCO CO.

MACDONALD'S

Gold Standard

"EXPORT"

Like a High Grade English Cigarette

FINEST VIRGINIA

CAMEL

TURKISH & DOMESTIC BLEND CIGARETTES

Raleigh CIGARETTES

REG. U.S. PAT. OFF.

Old Gold CIGARETTES

THE TREASURE OF THEM ALL

GERMANY'S LATEST WEAPON 1945

V29
VOLKSTURM IN ACTION

✠ MOST SECRET ✠

To: *HPLT BUHRAN*   A. Nr. *6343/*

                                              L. Nr. *144*

NOTICE

The watch found amongst your belongings is property of the ~~British Air Ministry~~
U. S. Army A. C.
and has therefore been confiscated according to War regulations.

Watch Nr.: *A.M. 6B/23/*

Auswertestelle West, *den 14/7 44*   *[signature]*

5510/44 Heidelberger Gutenberg-Druckerei GmbH. IX. 44.

INSIDE GERMANY

—I SAID "YOU'VE BEEN PROMOTED TO THE RANK OF CORPORAL IN THE VOLKSTURM

1944

Christmas Dinner

Potage Churchill
Devilled Ham à la Stalin
    Tito Sauce
Turkey à la Roosevelt
    Pommes Eisenhower
    Cabbage Patch
    Carrots Patton
Montgomery Pudding
Pudding Varsovienne
De Gaulle Sundae
Fromage Alexander
    Café Victoire
    Gâteau Noël

TOASTS

The King
Poland
Victory in 1945

PRIMA RESTAURANT
KRIEGSGEFANGENEN ONLY
GUT GOON FOOD

WEEKLY MENU
FEBRUARY & MARCH 1945

Monday	Potatoes & Swedes
Tuesday	Swedes & Potatoes
Wednesday	Das Brot
Thursday	Potatoes
Friday	Potatoes
Saturday	Potatoes
Sunday	Potatoes & Swedes EXTRA Goon Tea

STALAG LUFT 1
BARTH
POMMERANIA
DEUTSCHLAND KAPUT

GRAND
EASTER
LUNCHEON

MENU

Easter greeting eggs

Tartinnes à la Arct

Salade Polonaise

Crême de fromage

Grilled spam
roast potatoes
fried onions

Kriegie pudding

Gâteau à la Pentz

Coffée

Biscuits & cheese

Cigarettes

TOASTS

THE KING	by	S/L. H.R. De Belleroche
POLAND	by	S/L. G.M. Rothwell
BELGIUM	by	F/LT. J.A. Pentz
VICTORY	by	S/L. B. Arct

the life and death of the word

GOON

THIS IS HOW IT WAS BORN AND LIVED

When Walt Disney invented the "Goon" he little thought that the German nation would ever come to be known by that word in the language of Ps.O.W. Disney's "Goon" was a ridiculous looking figure with a prolific growth of fur on the legs. Their language was unintelligable and they were not credited with a superfluity of intelligence.

This "Goon" was ideally suited to the needs of Ps.O.W as a word for their captors.

AND THIS SHOWS HOW IT DIED...

Kriegsgefangenenlager Nr. 1, d.Lw.   Barth, den 2.7.44
        Gruppe II

To:The Senior American Officer North Compound,
   The Senior American Officer Main Compound,
   The Senior British Officer Main Compound,

Re: Use of the word "goon".
    The use of the word "goon" was granted to the Ps. o. W. by the Kommandant under the condition that this word would not have any dubious meaning.
    It has however, been reported to me that Ps. o. W. have been using the word "focking goon up", the meaning of which is beyond any doubt.
    Consequently the use of the word "goon up" or "goon" is prohibited, severest punishment being in future inflicted for any disobedience against this order.

                                           gez. Schroder
                                           Major u. Gruppenleiter.

ROOM 2

SIX PEOPLE ARE SUDDENLY PRECIPITATED INTO A ROOM WHERE THEY MUST EAT, SLEEP, AND LIVE TOGETHER, IN A CAMP SURROUNDED BY BARBED WIRE AND GUARDS, IN WHICH 10.000 OTHER MEN OF ALL NATIONALITIES ARE INCARCE= =RATED. THIS WAS THE FATE OF THE SIX IN ROOM 2.

THERE WERE THREE BRITISH, TWO POLISH AND ONE BELGIAN, ALL DIFFERING IN TEMPERAMENT, SPEECH, CUSTOMS, SENSE OF HUMOUR AND GEN= =ERAL METHOD OF LIVING. THE COMMON LANGUAGE USED, AND ABUSED, WAS ENGLISH. THROUGH ITS MEDIUM THE EXTEMPORANEOUS DECANTINGS OF THE SIX WERE CONVEYED INTO THE COLD, SMOKY, ATMOSPHERE WHICH USUALLY PREVAILED IN ROOM 2.

THE CONVERSATION WAS VARIED. THEY TALKED OF THE WAR, THEIR EXPERIENCES, AND A GREAT DEAL OF PURE UNADULTERATED DRIVEL. BUT ONE SUB= =JECT DISCUSSED MORE THAN ANYTHING ELSE, ESPECIALLY DURING THE STARVATION PERIOD DURING FEBRUARY AND MARCH 1945, WAS FOOD. THOUGH THERE WERE ARGUMENTS BY THE SCORE, ONE THING — FELLOWSHIP — BOUND THE SIX TOGETHER. THEY WERE ALL DETERMINED NOT TO ALLOW THE CONDITIONS TO "GET THEM DOWN" AND THOUGH TIMES WERE OFTEN PRETTY GRIM, THEY MADE THE BEST OF THEIR ENFORCED STAY IN STALAG LUFT I.

S/Ldr G. M. Rothwell

D.F.C. & Bar

"Watersplash" Bracken Bank Hutton Essex

England

In Oberursel's gloomy cell
For thirteen days I lived in Hell.
I thought of England, cool and green.
And all the happy days I'd seen.
We left those cells one welcome day;
Dan Holt and I were on our way!
Tho' times were grim we stuck together,
A friendship formed, to last forever.
And now our ways will have to part
I know that close beside my heart
Some happy memories will remain
Until the day we'll meet again.
Not very good, Dan, but original!! Yours age. Geoff.

S/Ldr H.R. De Belleroche

lo Whiteway Drive Heavitree Exeter

England

Day in the life of a Room L. Krieigie.
"Brew water up!" — this means 0800 hrs to
get up and attend roll call. there are 5 other
clocks in the room but only this one tells
the time. Roll Call is the only function of
a day for which a kind government bleeds
poor little rich factory workers 10/- in the £1.
to pay me 30/- and take away 15/- So what!
Return to room L. for seek duties.
the rest of the day is spent in talking about,
and thinking about, and sometimes even eating
Food. lets have a party!
Harry d.B.

S/Ldr C.G. De Moulin

D.F.C.   Croix de Guerre & 3 Palms

23 Rue Joseph Joppart Wavre

Belgium

Friendship is a great sentiment.
Forged in adversity, it is all the more dura-
ble. In times when one sometimes wonders
about humanity, it is good to find a mind
together with a heart ready to understand,
to share, to help.
We went through dark days together, and we
stuck it. Surely we can look towards the future,
and live assured that prosperity will not destroy,
but fortify, what was born in our German exile.

Charles.

F/Lt J.A. Pentz

Krzyż Walecznych   Croix de Guerre

Dobromil Lwów

Poland

F/Lt G.F. Stooks

Colingwood House Hawkhurst Kent

England

My first acquaintance with Dan was a speaking one only; This is explained by the fact that we conversed from adjacent cells in gaol. We had not cracked a crib or robbed a window but had got ourselves locked down by the brutal Hun at about the same time.

Our gaol acquaintance, however, was destined to become a prison friendship, as we eventually gyrated to the same room in "Temp R.A.F Station, Barth, Germany," alias Stalag Luft 1.

I sincerely hope that this friendship, started at Arnheim gaol in Sept '44 may continue for a great many peaceful years to come

Stooky

S/Ldr B.Arct
Virtuti Militari Krzyż Walecznych & 3 Bars

Warszawa

Poland

What can I write about
my own log-book?

You know there is a saying
That sunshine follows rain,
And sure enough you'll realise
That joy will follow pain;
Let courage be your password
Make fortitude your guide,
And then instead of grousing
Remember those who died.

THIS WAS WRITTEN BY AN ANO=
NYMOUS KRIEGIE ON THE WALL OF
HIS CELL WHILE DOING "SOLITARY"
IN THE COOLER.

BIG WHEELS

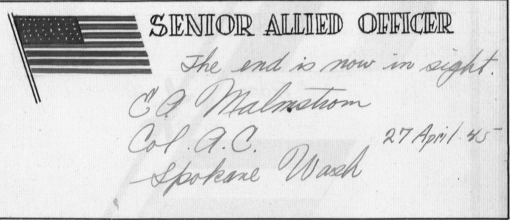

SENIOR ALLIED OFFICER

The end is now in sight.

C Q Malmstrom
Col. A.C.
Spokane Wash.

27 April 45

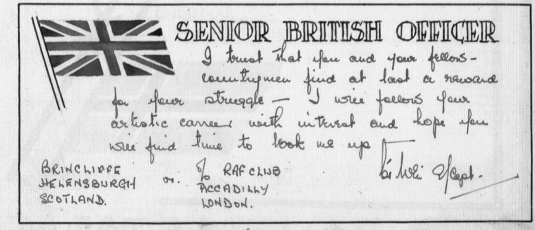

SENIOR BRITISH OFFICER

I trust that you and your fellow-countrymen find at last a reward for your struggle — I will follow your artistic career with interest and hope you will find time to look me up

G W Hislop Capt.

BRINCLIFFE
HELENSBURGH
SCOTLAND.

or.

% RAF CLUB
PICCADILLY
LONDON.

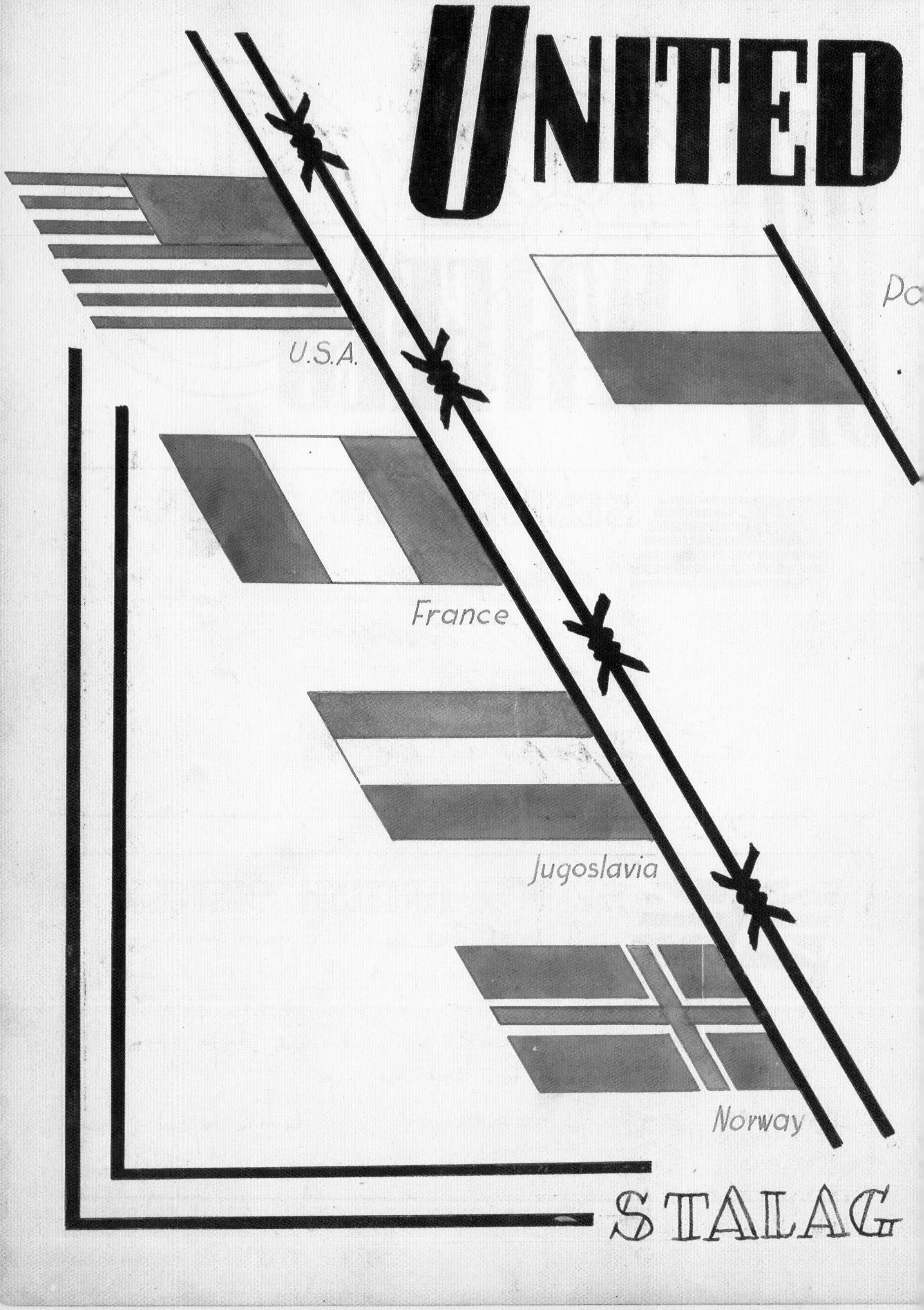

UNITED

U.S.A.

Po

France

Jugoslavia

Norway

STALAG

NATIONS

...und

Great Britain

Czechoslovakia

Belgium

Greece

LUFT 1

POLAND

Ku pamięci wspólnej niedoli   Rozkumiteem Bohdanowi
w stałag Luft I. Barth.   Byłek ze Śląska
          J. A. Pentz kpt.   14.IV.46.

Tydzień przed opuszczeniem   Ja wcale nie zamieram
"gościnnego Barth"   siedzieć tutaj jeszcze
wpisał Jasg Piewrzy Lech   cały tydzień
        14.IV.45.   Jan Piwiarek
                                      kpt.-pil.

Przed "odlotem" do Anglii
na pamiątkę wpisał się
        Herman Tadeusz
        19.IV.1945.

Kilka godzin? przed zakończeniem
się wojny. Wpisał się por. Kotarski St.

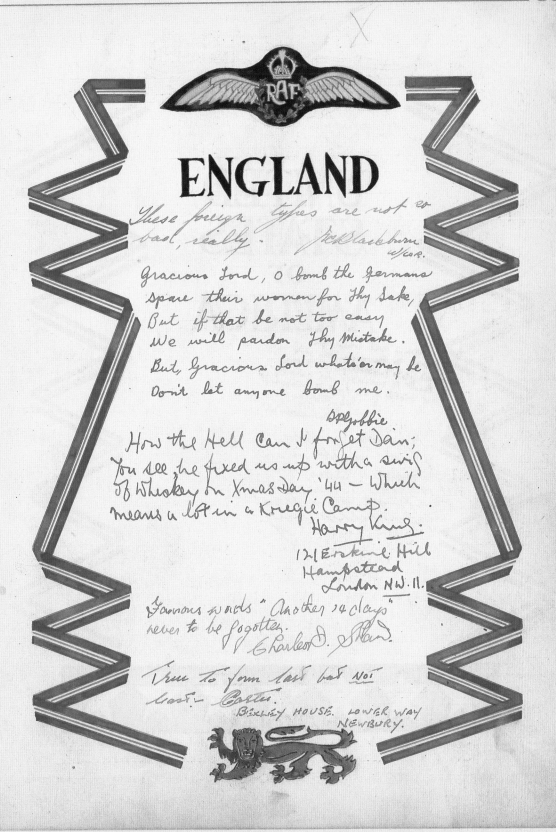

ENGLAND

These foreign types are not so
bad, really.   J.K.Blackburn
                              4/608.

Gracious Lord, O bomb the Germans
Spare their women for Thy Sake,
But if that be not too easy
We will pardon Thy Mistake.
But, Gracious Lord whate'er may be
Don't let anyone bomb me.

                    S.P.Gobbie

How the Hell can I forget Dan;
You see, he fixed us up with a swig
Of Whiskey on Xmas Day '44 — Which
means a lot in a Kriegie Camp.
                    Harry King.
                    121 Erskine Hill
                    Hampstead
                      London N.W.11.

Famous words "Another 14 days"
never to be forgotten.
              Charles D. Shand.

True to form last but not
least — Carter.
          BIXLEY HOUSE. LOWER WAY
                        NEWBURY.

UNITED STATES OF AMERICA

Hoping that when you come to America you will not fail to stop in at "Penguin Perch" to reminisce over gallons of Scotch of the days of Stalag Luft
John Widgton
3410 Q St.
Washington D.C.

My home will be yours while in America. Dan. The address is 228a E. Maple. Glendale. Cal.
Gerald D Crary

FRANCE

Vive la Pologne !
Philippe Millet . 5 Rue Henri de Bornier
CAPT. F.AF.C.# Paris 16°.

à Paris bientôt autour d'un
magnum de champagne
nous boirons à la Pologne et
à la France.
R. delegonzac LT F.A.F.L.
51 Rue Raynouard
Paris XVI eme

CZECHOSLOVAKIA

V upomínku na těžké
chvíle v zajetí prožívané s kamarády
Poláhami   vinye
                W/o.
        Frank Knap
Barth dne 15. dubna 1945
        Německo.

BELGIUM

Les ailes polonaises seront toujours
bienvenues dans le ciel Belge.

Avec l'expression de ma grande
admiration pour votre pays, et à vous,
mon cher Bohdan, l'assurance de ma
vive amitié. Charles du Moulin S/Ldr.

Dans les mauvaises heures comme
dans les bonnes, Polonais et Belges se
sont toujours rencontrés en frères luttant
pour un même idéal. Et même
dans ces dernières heures si remplies d'une
merveuse aspiration vers une
liberté prochaine c'est la même
fierté qui se traduit dans cette
amicale et peut-être dernière poignée
de mains à un ami.

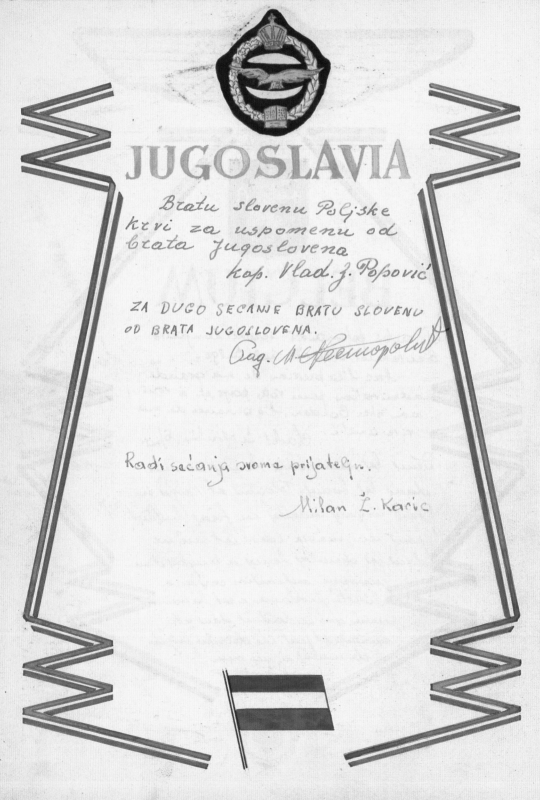

JUGOSLAVIA

Bratu slovenu Poljske
krvi za uspomenu od
brata Jugoslovena
        kap. Vlad. Ž. Popović

ZA DUGO SECANJE BRATU SLOVENU
OD BRATA JUGOSLOVENA.
        Gag. M. Kermopolut

Radi sećanja svoma prijatelju.

        Milan Ž. Karic

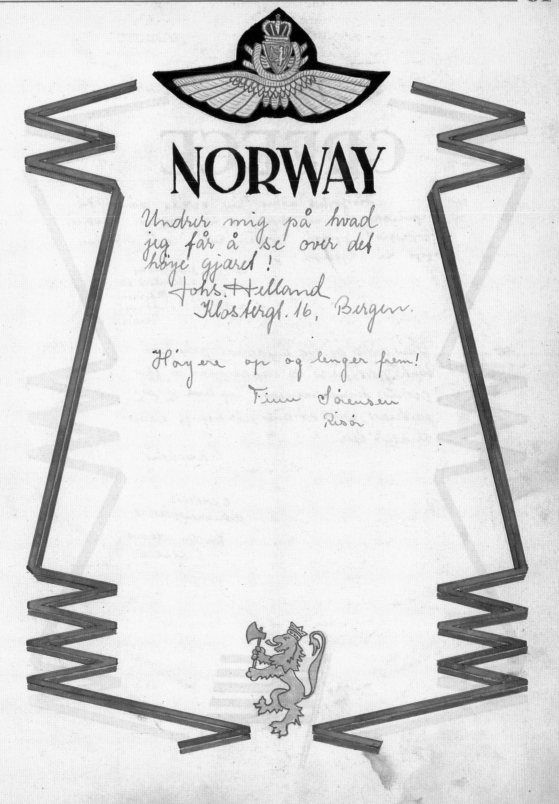

NORWAY

Undrer mig på hvad
jeg får å se over det
høye gjæret!
    Johs. Helland
        Klostergt. 16, Bergen.

Høyere op og lenger frem!

        Finn Sørensen
            Risør

GREECE

Ἀνοίγοντα αὐτὴν τὴν σελίδα πάντα θὰ
διερωτᾶσαι τί νὰ σημαίνῃ ἢ μᾶλλον ἐννοεῖ
τὴν μου γραφή. Τίποτε. Ἐκτὸς ἐὰν συμᾶσαι
κακὰ τὰ ἔγραψα.

Ν. Ε. Κοδωνᾶς.
Βrontou 59
Patissia
Athens
Greece

Ἐὰν αὗται αἱ δύο Ἑλληνικαὶ γραμμαὶ
συμβάλλουν ἰς τὸ νὰ παρουσιάσουν τὸ ἐξαι-
ρετικῶς διακοσμημένον 'Log Book' σου, ὡ-
ραιότερον, τοῦτο θὰ εἶναι μία μεγάλη εὐχαρί-
στησις δι' ἐμέ.

Ε. Καρύδης.

E. CARIDIS
Adrianoupoleos 13
Ymittos Athens
GREECE.

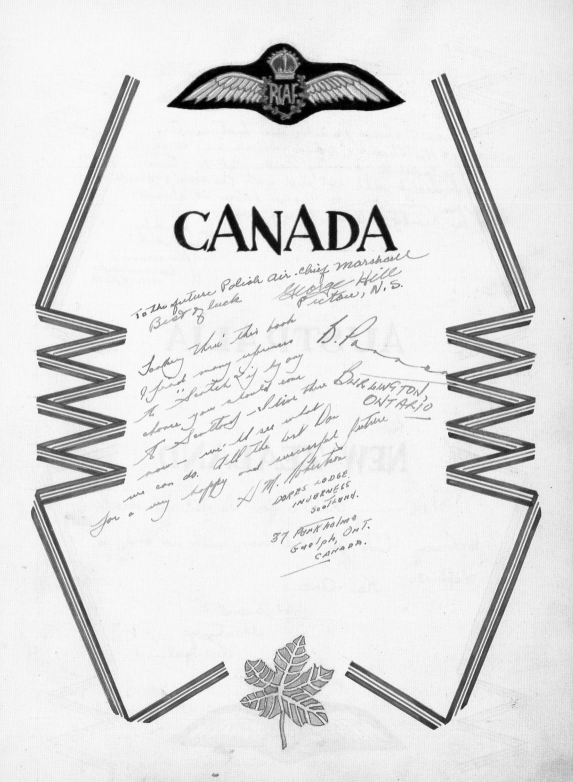

CANADA

Will always remember our first meeting,
& the Elegantes which believe me, were
a Godsend. Sincerely hope that our Kriegie
friendship will not end with the war, & should
you ever come to "Aussie" there is always
a hearty welcome to my home.

Brian L. Foley
Royal Hotel
Yarraman
Queensland
AUSTRALIA.

AUSTRALIA

NEW ZEALAND

With many thanks for the faithful escorts
to Norway. Wish you had been with us on
Sept. 12. Kai-Ora.

W Jacons.
Hastings
New Zealand.

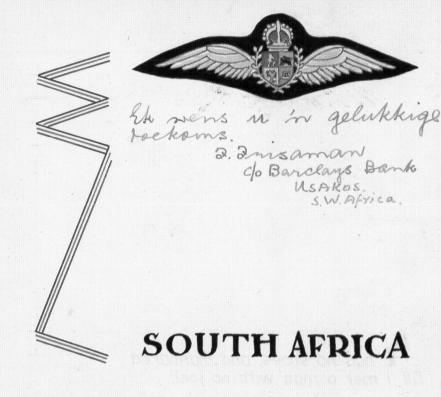

Ek wens u 'n gelukkige
toekoms.
    2. Inisaman
        c/o Barclays Bank
            USAKOS,
                S.W.Africa.

SOUTH AFRICA

RHODESIA

Zonke ena shalla mushi nange
nange.   S. McGibbon,
        124.B., Wilson Str.,
            Bulawayo,
                S. Rhodesia.

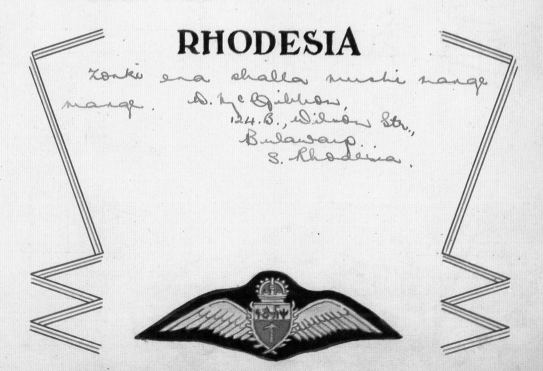

I had no shoes, and murmured
'Till I met a man with no feet.

ARABIAN PROVERB

STALAG LUFT FASHIONS 1944

When I first arrived in Stalag Luft 1 Camp I was struck by the enormous variety of dresses, caps, shoes and badges worn by Prisoners of War. Instead of seeing a crowd of normally uniformed men, one noticed American officers in R.A.F. uniforms, R.A.F. officers in American uniforms, officers in a mixture of both, Americans with huge drawings of their "ships" on the backs of their jackets, with bombs representing the number of "missions" to their credit, comical names painted on their jackets such as "Sweet Sue" or "Queen Texas". One American wore, embroidered on his breast, his rank, initials, name, home town, State and country. A few were to be seen in best blue trousers, tunics, greatcoats and ceremonial hats. One could walk around the camp for hours without seeing two people dressed alike.

That sight gave me an inspiration to draw some caricatures which I assembled in a series under the title "Stalag Luft Fashions 1944", copies of which can be seen on the following eight pages. Originals were drawn on thick, grey, paper, size 16 × 11 inches, in November 1944.

The series became rather popular amongst people visiting our tiny room 7 in Block II, where I then lived. I was asked many times to make copies of them, and as the currency in the camp was "D" bars and cigarettes, I have been paid in those items. Geoff Rothwell became my "Financial Adviser" and we soon fixed the price at 1200 cigarettes, six "D" bars or a typed cheque for £8 /payable on return to England/ per set. By the end of 1944 quite a large collection of cigarettes and chocolate had accumulated in the Red Cross boxes we used for cupboards.

I have made eleven sets of "Stalag Luft Fashions" and received for them 11.800 cigarettes, six „D" bars and £8 in cheque. Numerous drawings from the series were reproduced in peoples' Log Books but no charge was made for them.

Thus my old, pre-war, occupation, drawing, proved very useful and profitable in prison life, where so many people were desirous of obtaining souvenirs. I made enough cigarettes to last my friends and myself until the end of this war.

Other Series which I produced, served a dual purpose, by providing more cigarettes, and helping to keep my hand in as well. But that is another story—

What are these?
So withered and so wild in their attire
that look not like the inhabitants of earth
And yet are on't?

MACBETH

STALAG LUFT FASHIONS 1944

RAF CEREMONIAL DRESS

STALAG LUFT FASHIONS 1944

USAAF CEREMONIAL DRESS

STALAG LUFT FASHIONS 1944

POLISH AIR FORCE MESS KIT

STALAG LUFT FASHIONS 1944

CENSORED

STALAG LUFT FASHIONS 1944

SENIOR OFFICERS DRESS

STALAG LUFT FASHIONS 1944

RAF WINTER DRESS

STALAG LUFT FASHIONS 1944

RAF FANCY DRESS

STALAG LUFT FASHIONS 1999

THE OLDEST KRIEGIE

...If you can wait, and not be tired by waiting...

KIPLING

LIE IN THE DARK AND LISTEN

Lie in the dark and listen,
It's clear to-night so they're flying high.
Hundreds of them, thousands perhaps,
Riding the icy moonlit sky.
Men, machinery, bombs and maps,
Altimeters, guns and charts,
Sandwiches, coffee and fleece lined boots.
English saplings with English roots
Deep in the earth they've left below.
Lie in the dark and let them go,
Lie in the dark and listen.

Lie in the dark and listen,
They're going over in waves and waves,
High above mountains, rivers, streams,
Country church and little graves,
And little citizen's worried dreams.
Very soon they'll have reached the sea,
And far below them will lie the bays,
And shoals, and cliffs where they
Were taken for summer holidays.
Lie in the dark and let them go.
There's a world you'll never know,
Lie in the dark and listen.

Lie in the dark and listen,
City magnates and steel contractors,
Factory workers and politicians,
Self hysterical little actors,
Ballet dancers, reserved musicians
Safe in your warm civilian beds.
Count your blessings and count your sheep,
Life is passing above your heads.
Just turn over and go to sleep.
Lie in the dark and let them go,
Theirs' is a debt you'll forever owe.
Lie in the dark and listen.

Noel Coward

WAIT FOR ME

Wait for me, I will come back
Only wait... and wait,
Wait though rainclouds lowering black
Make you desolate;
Wait though winter snowstorms whirl,
Wait though summer's hot,
Wait though no one else will wait
And the past forgot:
Wait though from the distant front
Not one letter comes;
Wait though, though everyone who waits
Sick of it becomes.

Wait for me, I will come back
Pay no heed to those
Who'll so glibly tell you that
It is vain to wait,
Though my mother and my son
Think that I am gone,
Though my friends abandon hope
And back there at home
Rise and toast my memory
Wrapped in silence pained,
Wait! And when they drink toast
Heave your glass undrained.

Wait for me, I will come back
Though from death's own paws
Let the friends who did not wait
Think it chance, no more
They will never understand
Those who did not wait
How it was your waiting that
Saved me in the war,
And the reason I've come through
We shall know, we two;
Simply this: You waited as
No one else could do.

Translation of a Russian poem

LETTERS
FROM OUR BELOVED ONES

The following are actual extracts from letters received by Prisoners of War in this camp.
For obvious reasons I have not disclosed their names.

I have been living with a private since you were missing, but please don't stop allotment as he does not make as much as you...

/R.A.F. SERGEANT FROM WIFE/

I am filing a divorce. Mother and I have discussed it and, since it is four years since you went down, we decided it was best...

/R.A.F W/O FROM WIFE/

We are not sending parcels as we hear you can buy all you want in stores near the camp...

/LT. B.T. FROM HOME/

I am longing for you to return so I can make our divorce final. I've lived with an armament worker for some time. He really is sweet...

/LT. T.M. FROM WIFE/

Please have a photo taken to send to me...

/LT. T.L. FROM WIFE/

> **D**on't bother to hurry home as I am living with an American and having a lovely time. I am having his baby soon, but forgive me — Mother has. He is sending you cigarettes...
>
> /F/O A.K. FROM WIFE/

> **A**m enclosing a calendar. It will be useful as it has several years on it...
>
> /LT. L.P.B. FROM AUNT/

> **I** hear you need nothing as you get so much food and clothing where you are. Could you send a package with stockings if possible...
>
> /LT. G.H.K. FROM WIFE/

Now I come to the "Plum" of the collection. This one, I think, is difficult to beat and is written by the unfortunate prisoner's fiancée.

> **C**onsider our friendship at an end. I would sooner marry a 1944 hero than a 1939 coward...

The recipient of this letter was severely wounded in the face after a 20 m.m. explosive cannon shell had burst in the cockpit of his aircraft. He was exploded from the blazing aircraft and spent four anxious months in hospital awaiting news from home. He was highly commended by his crew for bravery and leadership.

BELIEVE IT OR NOT

The fiancée of a P.o.W. wrote and told him that it was all off and he might at least have died for his country.

The P.o.W. who got a letter from his wife saying she was going to have a baby by an Army Major, but everything would be alright and the Major was going to send him cigarettes regularly.

An American P.o.W. received a letter from a girl saying he was going to be a father and he didn't even know her.

A Canadian P.o.W. received a letter from his wife asking if he was willing to lend his golf clubs to a German P.o.W. in Canada, and who, when he refused, was asked to resign from his golf club on the grounds of being unsporting to a gallant enemy.

A P.o.W. wrote and thanked an old lady for a knitted scarf which he had received from the Red Cross and got an angry letter back saying it had never been intended for a P.o.W. but for someone who was fighting for his country.

A P.o.W. who had a white feather sent him by the widow of one of his crew.

The P.o.W. who received a letter from his fiancée saying that after four years she could wait for him no longer and had married his father.

A P.o.W. who received a letter from his wife saying she was enclosing a photograph of herself in the nude. A note from the German censor explained that the photograph had been confiscated.

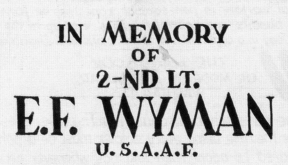

IN MEMORY
OF
2-ND LT.
E.F. WYMAN
U.S.A.A.F.

WHO WAS SHOT
WHILST ENTERING HIS BARRACKS
BY A GERMAN GUARD
DURING AN AIR RAID WARNING

ON
MARCH 18-TH
1945

TO ALL PRISONERS OF WAR!

THE ESCAPE FROM PRISON CAMPS IS NO LONGER A SPORT!

Germany has always kept to the Hague Convention and only pu=
=nished recaptured prisoners of war with minor disciplinary punishment.
Germany will still maintain these principles of international law.

But England has besides fighting at the front in an honest manner
instituted an illegal warfare in non-combat zones in the form of gangster
commandos terror bandits and sabotage troops even up to the frontiers of Germany.

They say in a captured secret and confidential English military pamphlet:

THE HANDBOOK
OF MODERN IRREGULAR
WARFARE

"...the days when we could practise the rules of sportsman=
=ship are over. For the time being every soldier must be a potential gangster
and must be prepared to adopt their methods whenever necessary."

"The sphere of operations should always include the enemy's
own country, any occupied territory and in certain circumstances such neutral
countries as he is using as a source of supply."

ENGLAND HAS WITH THESE INSTRUCTIONS OPENED UP
A NON MILITARY FORM OF GANGSTER WAR!

Germany is determined to safeguard her home=
land and especially her war industry and provisional centres
for the fighting fronts. Therefore it has become necessary to
create strictly forbidden zones called death zones, in which
all unauthorised trespassers will be immediately shot on sight.

Escaping prisoners of war, entering such death
zones will certainly lose their lives. They are therefore in con=
=stant danger of being mistaken for enemy agents or sabota=
ge groups.

URGENT WARNING IS GIVEN AGAINST MAKING FUTURE
ESCAPES!

In plain English: Stay in the camp where you
will be safe! Breaking out of the camp now is a damned
dangerous act.

THE CHANCES OF PRESERVING YOUR LIFE ARE ALMOST
NIL!

All police and military guards have been gi=
ven the most strict orders to shoot on sight all suspected
persons.

ESCAPING FROM PRISON CAMPS

HAS CEASED AS A SPORT!

COPY

VERBOTEN

The second series of sketches I produced in Stalag Luft 1 were those shown on the next six pages. The idea originated by the deluge of German orders and warnings pointing out the deadly danger of attempting escape from prison camps. They threatened to shoot without warning (and they did) at anybody breaking those orders and they improved their system of guarding us so much, that it was practically impossible to penetrate the double row of barbed wire, avoiding the bloodthirsty dogs within the camp, evade the machine gun fire from the towers around the camp, miss the numerous patrols outside and in immediate surroundings, get across Germany and land safely in friendly territory. And all that would have to be done during the hard winter frost and in the deep snow, since I only arrived here in October.

The only means of escape then were those shown on following pages. If any of the readers of this book finds himself in a prison camp in similar circumstances to ours, he may try. Good luck.

I have made 6 copies of „Verboten" and numerous single sketches in people's Log Books and received for them 2700 cigarettes, 4 "D" bars and £12 in cheques.

VERBOTEN

VERBOTEN

VERBOTEN

VERBOTEN

VERBOTEN

*I*t is by the goodness of God that we have possession of three unspeakable precious things— Freedom of speech, freedom of conscience, and the prudence of using neither.

M. TWAIN

MAIL

From the time he enters the prison camp every P.o.W. yearns for the day when he will receive his first letter. Mail is the one and only link we have with the world outside the barbed wire. For months we wait anxiously, hoping feverishly that one of those letters in the newly-arrived sacks will bring us glad news from home. We are disappointed numerous times – friends and room mates who are luckier than we, are envied as they joyfully talk of the contents of those blue & white sheets.

Generally, the first letter is received four to six months after arrival at a permanent camp but some are lucky and receive letters before then, others, more unfortunate, go for considerably longer periods without news from home.

MAIL I RECEIVED

September 1944	NIL
October 1944	NIL
November 1944	NIL
December 1944	NIL
January 1945	NIL
February 1945	NIL
March 1945	NIL
April 1945	NIL
May 1945	NIL

These Pages Are For
MEN ONLY

LADIES WILL NOT LOOK
WOMEN SHOULD NOT LOOK
-------- CAN LOOK IF THEY CHOOSE

You Have Been Warned

HEARD IN OUR KRIEGIE CAMP ANY HOUR OF ANY DAY

"Some new kriegies in!"
"Anybody off Battles?"
"When do they say the war will be over at home?"
"What are things like at home?"
"Is there plenty of booze in England?"
"How long have you been down?"
"I suppose they knew all about you at Oberürsel?"
"How long were you in the cooler?"
"Rations up"
"Come and get it"
"Come on, Joe!"
"Bowls up for soup"
"Swedes up"
"Any gash?"
"Morgen"
"Come in"
"Enemy up for roll call!"
"F..k their horrible luck"
"2-nd bugle, everybody out for roll call!"
"Tank you. Plisse let dem stand at ease"
"Enemy approaching barracks"
"Henry up"
"Let's have a brew"
"It's that bloody awful earthy Goon soup again!"
"You can stuff it up your arse!"
"How long do you give it now?"
"Red Cross parcels up!"

"Any "D" bars to sell?"
"Dankes very firkin"
    "Whadyasay?"
"What's that?"
    "Goon shit"
"Whadyaknow?"
    "Not a dam thing"
"Take it easy"
    "Get off the pit"
"Water's off"
    "Turn the lights on, you Square headed bastards!"
"You are round the firkin"
    "What do you think of the news?"
"He's completely round the bend"
    "Deutschland kaput"
"Hubba, hubba!"
    "How long do the spuds have to last?"
"Gosh, I'm hungry!"
    "Hard luck!"
"It's as good as over"
    "Germany's going for a shit"
"On guard"
    "What's your date?"
"Racket!"
    "What's the gen?"
"Got any rumours?"
    "Had any mail yet?"
"Is the communique up yet?"
    "Brew water up"
"2o men for showers"
    "How's the morale?"
"Das focking brot"
    "Let's have a party"
"You've had it"
    "What is your kriegie number?"
"I had to get up 8 times for a pee last night"
    "The bastards are searching Block 6"
"I heard a good shit-house rumour"
    "I wonder if we'll get any lights tonight!"
"Air Raid Warning!"
    "Let's have a snack"
"Firkin schön"
    "Why don't these stupid bastards pack in?!!!"

MEN ONLY

GRAVY & BROT

COMPOSED AND PERFORMED IN BARRACK 11 BY LT. STUTZER USAAF

I've travelled this Deutschland wide over
I've stopped at all Stammlager Lufts
Some were good, some were bad,
Some were different,
And others the best that they had.
Now this last one I stopped at
Was a lulu,
So clean and fine and neat
But all wasn't Rotten Cross Parcels
Wait till you hear what we had to eat.
Now on Montag we had brot and gravy,
On Dienstag 'twas gravy and brot,
On Mitwoch and Donnestag we had gravy on toast
Which is nothing but gravy on brot.
On Freitag I went to the Hauptmann
To ask him for something instead,
So on Samstag in the morgen
By way of a change
We had gravy without any bread.

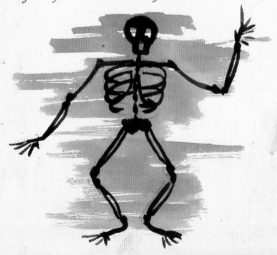

MY BETS

Whilst in captivity I made numerous bets as to when the war would end. It was agreed that the end of the war would be taken as the date it was officially announced by the B.B.C., or in the event of our camp being liberated, the date the first kriegie left to be repatriated.

Each of the bets was for one bottle of whisky payable on return to England.

Details of the bets were as follows:—

F/O Kanewsky Czech Air Force 10.9.1944	Kanewsky bets that the war will end before 15.10.1944	I won
F/Lt Stooks R.A.F. 10.9.1944	Stooks bets that the war will end before 1.11.1944	I won
S/L De Moulin 20.1.1945	De Moulin bets that the war will end before 15.5.1945	I lost
F/Lt Stooks 20.1.1945	Stooks bets that the war will end before 15.5.1945	I lost
F/Lt De Large Polish Air Force 1.2.1945	De Large bets that the war will not end before 21.6.1945	I won
F/Lt Kotlarz Polish Air Force 5.2.1945	Kotlarz bets that the war will not end before 21.6.1945	I won
F/Lt Winiarek Polish Air Force 3.3.1945	Winiarek bets that the war will end before 1.5.1945	I won
S/L De Moulin Belgian Air Force 15.3.1945	De Moulin bets that the war will end before 1.4.1945	I won

You shall judge of a man by his foes as well as by his friends.

J. CONRAD

The five sketches on the following pages were originally intended to convey some idea of prison camp life. When the idea germinated, I was extremely busy copy-ing my "Stalag Luft Fashions" and "Verboten" for various people, and the production of this new series was delayed and never fully materialised.

Nevertheless some of these sketches achieved popularity and I was asked many times to reproduce them in peoples' log books. These log books became a nightmare to me. As soon as people realised that I could draw, they began bringing their books to me, asking me to do "anything at all". At times I had, piled on my table, as many as fifteen logs, which rather disturbed my nor-mal routine. But it was so difficult to refuse, and somehow I managed to cope.

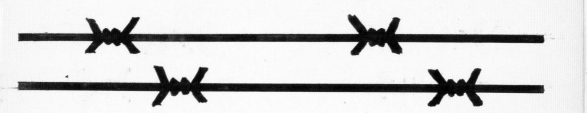

STALAG LUFT LIBRARY

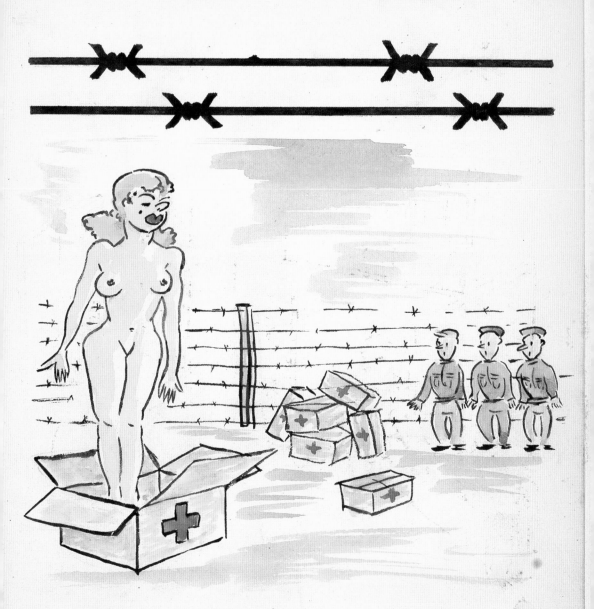

GOOD OLD ENGLAND

Oh, the years we waste and the tears we waste
And the work of our head and hand
Belong to the woman who did not know
And did not understand.

R. KIPLING

KRIEGIE'S recipes

POLISH SALAD

½ red or white cabbage
12 potatoes
4 onions / if available through trading
4 carrots   with Goons
1 tin Salmon or Pilchard
Vinegar /quantity dependant on Goons
                         by trading
Salt and pepper

Peel potatoes, slightly undercook and slice. Shred cabbage, chop carrots and onions and mix all together in a bowl with fish. Pour on vinegar, add some salt and pepper and leave for a few hours to bring out flavour. Serves three Kriegies or six ordinary persons.

POTATO FLAPJACKS

12 potatoes
2 tablespoons Klim
2 tablespoons flour, if available
1 tin Bully Beef
2 onions, if available through tra=
             ding with Goons

Grate potatoes raw, drain, add Klim, flour and chopped onions, mix with bully.
Fry in hot distilled margarine.

CREAMED SALMON

1 tin Salmon
½ tin cheese
3 tablespoons Klim
2 table-spoons margarine

Melt cheese, margarine and Klim in frying pan with a little water. When melted, add Salmon and mix thoroughly, stirring until hot. Serve as a spread on toast/Goon brot/ or as a sauce on mashed pota=
                              =toes

SPAM AND CHEESE RISSOLES

1 tin Spam
1 tin Cheese
Onions, if available through trading
                with Goons

Slice Spam and cheese. On one slice of Spam place a slice of onion, slice of cheese, another slice of onion and top with another slice of Spam. Bake in oven/if coal is available/ until cheese melts and Spam is crisp and brown.

ROTHWELL'S RIB-STICKER OR DAS KRIEGIE BROT PUDDING

1 Klim tin bread crusts
½ packet prunes /stoned/
½ packet raisins
4 table-spoons margarine
7 table-spoons sugar
2 table-spoons Klim

Chop prunes. Cut crusts into small cubes and toast in oven until hard and brown. Soak in a solution of Klim until soggy and then mash. Add other ingredients and mix thoroughly. Bake in a greased basin. When top is brown and crisp, invert and remove on to a baking tin. When brown all over, serve with apple sauce. Last item is dependant on Canadian Red Cross Parcels or trading prospects with Goons. Satisfies 6 Kriegies, serves 15 ordinary people.

PENTZ'S EXTRA SPECIAL CAKE

2 packets biscuits
1 —,— cereal
⅓ loaf dried Goon bread
3 tablespoons Klim
6 tablespoons powdered sugar
1 packet stoned & chopped prunes
3 tablespoons distilled marge
FILLING:
½ packet stoned & chopped prunes
⅓ packet raisins
1 tablespoon margarine
½ pint milk
ICING:
4 tablespoons Goon marge
3   —"—   Klim
5   —"—   powdered sugar
1   —"—   cocoa
1   —"—   cold water

Mix ingredients, adding milk gradually, until a stiff, but not too wet, consistency is obtained. Bake in a greased Klim tin baking pan.

Boil filling mixture on a slow fire until thick, and cover the cake.

Mix icing ingredients in a bowl and beat vigourously, until thick and creamy. Spread on top of filling.
N.B.
If possible don't eat the cake as soon as it is baked. It obtains a better flavour if kept until the following day. This practice, however, was never adopted in Room 2.

ROUND THE BEND

An American P.o.W in Stalag Luft 1 was seen watering the garden during a rain-storm.

An Englishman made a bet that if the war was not over by Christmas 1944, he would eat his Christmas dinner in the outdoor latrine. It was cold and frosty, with snow lying thick on the ground, when a table, laden with food, was taken into the draughty lavatory. The over-optimistic Kriegie took up his position on one of the seats and went through the menu before an amused audience.

An Englishman was seen outside the barracks when a strong wind was causing a miniature sandstorm, toasting a slice of bread over a Klim tin containing a glowing lump of coal.

An American made a bet that if the war was not over by 11.00 hrs. on Christmas Day 1944, he would kiss the bare posterior of his collegue in the middle of the Parade grounds. At 10.45 hrs. a bugle was sounded and a stage was erected, around which a huge crowd formed a circle. The winner's trousers were lowered and a "Second" carefully washed and powdered the part which was to receive this gesture of affection. With due ceremony the kiss was delivered, while icy winds swept across the sports field. The two prisoners returned to their Christmas dinner wondering who had come off best — winner or loser.

Remember me when I am gone away,
Gone far away into the silent land,
When you can no more hold me by the hand,
Nor I half turn to go, yet turning stay.
Remember me when no more, day by day,
You tell me of our future that you planned,
Only remember me, you understand
It will be late to counsel then or pray.
Yet if you should forget me for a while
And afterwards remember, do not grieve:
For if the darkness and corruption leave
A vestige of the thoughts that once I had,
Better by far you should forget and smile,
Than that you should remember and be sad.

CHRISTINE ROSSETTI

KRIEGIE RETURNS

The final series of sketches were drawn when the fronts were 70 kms. apart, Allied troops were poised on the Elbe ready to deliver the "Coup de grace", Russians were pouring into the country between Oder and Elbe and the camp was alive with conjecture on how and when we would be liberated.

We had, in the last seven months, so adapted ourselves to "Kriegie" routine, that I often wondered how some of the prisoners, who had been in captivity for two, three, four and in some cases five years, would behave when they returned to their homes and civilization.

The Series is composed of some of the situations which could arise if a "Kriegie" forgot himself when repatriated. None of these sketches were sold, since I was working entirely on my own log book in an endeavour to complete it before returning to England.

KRIEGIE RETURNS

— I'M AFRAID SIR, WE DON'T SELL
FUR COATS FOR BARS OF CHOCOLATE —

KRIEGIE RETURNS

-BUT DARLING, IT'S MY MOTHER!-

KRIEGIE RETURNS

—YOU NEEDN'T GO OUT FOR THOSE THINGS, DARLING!—

KRIEGIE RETURNS

—BUT YOU DON'T HAVE TO DO YOUR OWN "DHOBYING", THE LAUNDRY DO IT!—

KRIEGIE RETURNS

—DO I HAVE TO TELL YOU EVERY TIME THAT WE DON'T PUNCTURE OUR TINS HERE!—

KRIEGIE RETURNS

-FOR HEAVEN'S SAKE DON'T TOUCH THE WIRE OR THE POSTERN WILL SHOOT!!!-

POST MORTEM

Everything comes to an end, so did the war, and all of us Kriegies at last found ourselves back among civilised people, regaining the freedom we had missed so much.

I do not regret now the time I spent in Stalag Luft I, as I had a chance to see how it all looked, I met a lot of interesting people and learnt a good deal about the Germans.

In addition I had an opportunity to make this logbook, which gave me a lot of thrills and great satisfaction, especially when the Goons were furiously searching my room. However they never found it, otherwise it would never be here, in England.

BARTH

HARD TIMES

Vol 1   No. 1   LAST 1   SATURDAY MAY 5th 1945   PRICE 1 D- BAR.

Editor: F/L E. R. INKPEN   Assoc: 1st Lt N. GIDDINGS   Publisher: 1st Lt D. MacDONALD   Printing: F/LT J. D. WHITE

RUSSKY COME!

As seen by LOWELL BENNET, I. N. S. War Correspondent.

RELIEVED!

Colonel Zemke inten-
ded to write this appre-
ciation of the relief of
Stalag Luft I, but unfor-
tunately   necessary
duties have made this
impossible.   He has,
in his own words, "ta-
ken a powder" to make
final arrangements with
the relieving Soviet
forces.

It is therefore my pri-
vilege to introduce this
Memorial Edition of the
BARTH HARD TIMES.

During the successes,
reverses and stagnant
periods   encountered
during this struggle,
our newspaper has
faithfully recorded the
German war commu-
niques and expanded
upon them in capable
editorials.

With the redemption of
a continent, our exile
is ended. Our barb-
bound community will
soon be a memory. So,
on behalf of Colonel
Hubert Zemke and
myself, to all our fel-
low-kriegies: G O O D
L U C K !

G./C. C. T. Weir.

WHAT D'YE KNOW- JOE!!

BRAITHWAITE FINDS UNCLE JOE

Contacts Russian Infantryman at Crossroads
Five miles South of Stalag One.

Major Braithwaite and Sgt Korson, our
Stalag scouts, raced out to a cross-roads
5 miles south of Barth with the order,
"find Uncle Joe". This was 8 p.m., May 1.

They searched southward, defying a
rumored Russian curfew which was about
as brief and emphatic as their own order:
"EVERYONE stay put; anyone seen
moving will be shot on sight."

Meanwhile, Wing Commander Blackburn's
telephone crew were ringing numbers
in Stralsund, hoping a Russian would

answer the phone and we could break
the big news of our presence. "Try the
mayor," they asked the girl (who was still
working Barth's phone exchange). "Not
a chance," said she. "Barth's mayor pois-
oned himself and Stralsund's mayor has
sprouted wings."

Scouts Braithwaite and Korson pushed
on 3 miles. The scenery: thousands of
people everywhere, sitting down, waiting.

LIFE AND DEATH OF A GERMAN TOWN

TENSE MOMENTS WHILE ALLIES TAKE CONTROL

An air of tension hung over the camp for many days. The presence of the English and American armies on the Elbe and the Russian encirclement of Berlin made everyone feel that the end must be near. The commencement of a new Russian drive across the lower Oder toward the Baltic ports finally increased the tension to an almost unbearable pitch. Panic reigned in the Vorlager. No German had any more interest in guarding the prisoners, but only in saving his own life. Confidential reports were hurriedly burnt — and copies of "Mein Kampf" went to swell the flames.

Conference with the Kommandant

Finally, late in the afternoon, the Senior British and American officers were called to a conference with the German camp Kommandant Colonel Warnstedt. They were told that orders had been received to move the whole camp westward. Colonel Zemke stated he was not willing to move at all, and asked in that case what the German attitude would be. The Commandant replied that he would not tolerate bloodshed in the camp; if we did not intend to move, he and his men would evacuate themselves and leave us in sole possession of the camp. When the Germans left it would be up to us to take over the camp peacefully and assume full control.

At approximately 1 A.M. on April 30 Major Steinhauer informed Group Captain Weir and Colonel Zemke that the Germans had evacuated the camp, leaving it in our charge. When the camp woke up in the morning it was to find itself no longer under armed guard and comparatively free.

Where are the Russians?

Our next problem was to establish contact with the Russian forces. It was decided to send out something in the nature of a recco patrol. An American Major, a British Officer speaking German, and an American Officer speaking Russian, set out with the German in the auto which was equipped with an American flag on one fender and a white flag on the other, to investigate the real situation in Barth and then proceed to the main Stralsund – Rostock road, some 15 kilometers south of the camp, to wait there for any signs of Russian spearheads or of the proximity of the front line. The first patrol returned in the early evening. Still no sign or news of the Russian Army, but they were coming!

Russian Contact (con. from Page 1)
Every house draped with red flags (who said the Germans weren't chameleons?). Suddenly, there was Uncle Joe — or one of his ambassadors: a chunky little Dead End guy who loomed up and flashed a variety of lethal weapons and a cacophony of Slavic language.

"Engliski", shouted the scouts.

"Never mind the words", said Joe's man, "this isn't Dulag" or something like that in Russian. And, without ceremony they went to the nearest Russian officer. It was 1st Lt. Alec Nick Karmyzoff, infantryman from Tula (you oughta see that written in Russian!) He'd fought his way from Stalingrad — three years across Russia, Poland and Germany — to the relief of Stalag Luft I.

Toasts are Drunk.

Karmyzoff came in the main gate. Commanding Officers Zemke and Weir received him. Schnapps seared kriegie throats — glasses smashed Hitler's picture, the barracks jiggled with cheering and back-pounding. Toasts were drunk: " To the destruction of Germany — she will never rise again! And to our solid and enduring friendship." Karmyzoff went to the Russian barracks (our co-kriegies) — told them about himself, their army and the new life that was beginning. Thus the first contact. Karmyzoff bedded down on the floor — "Rather the floor than a German bed," said he. BBC announced Hitler dead; kriegies heard the "Hit Parade" from home; the excitement was exhausting. — But what an experience!

QUAKING BARTH BURGHERS BOW BEFORE REDS

As Russian tanks rumbled Northwards on the cobblestone roads from Stralsund, as Russian cavalry and guerilla troops tore hell bent for the Baltic, as the spluttering German radio flashed a staccato of place names that had gone under in the Red rip tide, Barth became an open city and an open grave. The few Americans who had been in town on camp chores from Stalag I knew that the life of Barth was a living death. We had seen the streets peopled by children and octogenarians, we had noticed that all males were either lame, halt, or blind; we had stared into empty shop windows, and we had seen the soldiers of the master race straggle back from the fronts dazed, whipped, harbingers of the ruin that stalked the streets of German towns. By April 30, this year of grace, the good burghers of Barth turned their faces to the wall and stopped hoping.

LET 'EM EAT CAKE

Life had not been good. In the bakery shop where the camp brot was made hung a sign; cake is not sold to Jews or Poles. It failed to explain that cake was not sold to the supermen either. There was no cake. But there were good things to eat in the larders of Barth, baking powder requisitioned from Holland, Nestles milk commandeered from Denmark, wines looted from the cellars of France, spaghetti and noodles hijacked from Italy, Worcestershire sauce which had trickled through mysteriously from England, olive oil drained from Greece, in short, all types of blood from the turnip of Europe. If Mussolini considered the Mediterranean his sea, Hitler considered the world his oyster and was trying to serve it up to the Reich on the half shell.

A House of Cards

As the first explosions from the flak school reverberated under the sullen Baltic sky, the new order toppled on Barth like a house of cards. Red flags and white sheets began to appear in the windows of the ginger bread houses. Flight was futile and the old stood querously on their door steps, wringing gnarled hands and weeping. Pictures of Hitler were torn down and scattered like confetti. Two German children came wailing into the bakery shop. They had heard American airmen ate little boys and mother said the day of reckoning was at hand.

Barth, like the whole of Deutschland-über-alles Germany, was on its knees in terror. But mayhem did not materialize. Wine, not blood, flowed through the streets. We got drunk.